THE BAYOU BULLETIN

Bed-and-Breakfast To Open!

Ms. Annabelle Delacroix Rowland, daughter of Senator Philip Delacroix, has become Bayou Beltane's newest businesswoman. Ms. Rowland, who, with her son, has recently returned to Saint Tammany parish after a sixteen-year absence, announced her plans yesterday to renovate the Portier House and open it to the public as a bed-and-breakfast.

The Portier House, once the family home of Mr. and Mrs. Henry Portier, is one of the finest examples of Victorian architecture in this area. Its distinctive style, with turretlike structures on both front corners of the house, almost gives it the appearance of a castle. "I was always drawn to this house," admitted Ms. Rowland. "It seemed as if it belonged in a fairy tale, where dreams actually came true for those who lived inside. I guess in my case, they already have."

The Portier House is currently under renovation and is due to open for business in approximately three months' time.

Sandy Steen is acknowledged
as the author of this work.

ISBN 0-373-82566-8

SON OF THE SHERIFF

Copyright © 1998 by Harlequin Books S.A.

Printed in U.S.A.

DELTA JUSTICE

Son of the Sheriff

SANDY STEEN

Harlequin Books

TORONTO • NEW YORK • LONDON
AMSTERDAM • PARIS • SYDNEY • HAMBURG
STOCKHOLM • ATHENS • TOKYO • MILAN
MADRID • WARSAW • BUDAPEST • AUCKLAND

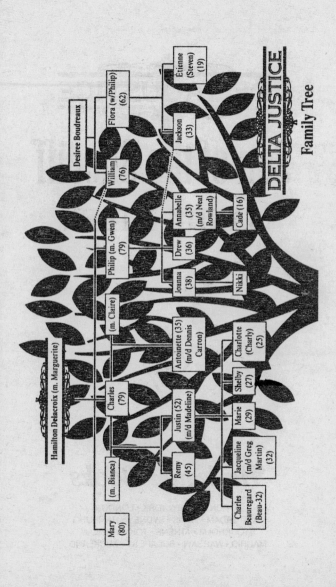

DELTA JUSTICE

Family Tree

Hamilton Delacroix (m. Marguerite)

Mary (80) — (m. Bianca)

Charles (79) — (m. Claire)

Desiree Boudreaux

William (76)

Flora (w/Philip) (62)

Philip (m. Gwen) (79)

Remy (45)

Justin (m/d Madeline) (52)

Antoinette (35) (m/d Dennis Carron)

Joanna (38)

Drew (36)

Annabelle (35) (m/d Neal Rowland)

Jackson (33)

Étienne (Steven) (19)

Charles Beauregard (Beau - 32)

Jacqueline (m/d Greg Martin) (32)

Marie (29)

Shelby (27)

Charlotte (Charly) (25)

Nikki

Cade (16)

CAST OF CHARACTERS

Annabelle Delacroix—Youngest daughter of Philip Delacroix. Newly divorced, she's come home to start over. The last thing she expected was for the past to catch up with her....

Jake Trahan—Sixteen years ago, he lost the only woman he'd ever loved. Now he's got a second chance. But will he be able to look past her deception?

Philip Delacroix—Annabelle's tyrannical father, a Louisiana state senator.

Cade Rowland—Annabelle's fifteen-year-old son. He's not happy about leaving the only home he's ever known...and the only father.

Ty Trahan—Jake's fourteen-year-old son. After undergoing extensive medical treatment, Ty can use a friend. And he finds one...in his brother.

Dear Reader,

Like you, I love a good romance, especially ones where the hero and heroine find their way back to each other after a long separation. And when the love rekindled is a first love, it's even more special.

Sixteen years ago, Annabelle Delacroix was young and desperately in love with Jake Trahan, a boy her father considered extremely unsuitable. She made a mistake and has kept a secret locked in her heart ever since. Now, after a bad divorce, she's come home, determined to start over and make a new life for herself and her fifteen-year-old son, Cade. But the biggest obstacle to starting a new life may be an old love. Jake Trahan, former sheriff of Saint Tammany parish, now chief of police, never expected Annabelle to walk back into his life. When she does, he decides he won't make the same mistake twice.

I hope you enjoy *Son of the Sheriff*, my final contribution to the DELTA JUSTICE continuity series. And be sure not to miss any of the upcoming books in the program. There are all kinds of secrets that have yet to see the light of day.

Sincerely,

Sandy Steen

CHAPTER ONE

"DAMN," JAKE TRAHAN muttered when he caught the red light at the intersection of the old Covington road and the main highway north into Bayou Beltane. He rubbed the knot of tension at the back of his neck. His day had begun before sunrise with a call about a drunk driver almost plowing through the window of the convenience store near the golf course. This was followed by a series of small but demanding problems at the station that had to be dealt with before he could leave to take his son to the hospital for his scheduled treatment.

God, he was tired. Clear-to-the bone weary. As soon as the thought formed in his mind, he was ashamed of it. What was a little fatigue compared to what his son was going through? What was a little tension compared to surgery to remove a brain tumor?

The days Ty went in for chemotherapy meant endless hours of waiting as the lifesaving chemicals made the slow trip through his lanky young body. As usual, Ty took it better than Jake did, stubbornly insisting the chief of police of Bayou Beltane needed to be out catching criminals instead of hanging around a hospital where he couldn't do anything, anyway. But like father, like son, and Jake was every bit as determined to stay. Today had been an exception. He had to transfer a prisoner to New Orleans and couldn't assign the task to anyone else.

"No sweat, Dad," Ty had told him. "I'm going to watch the video of the Dodgers game you brought me. Gotta start getting ready for the season even before I get on the field."

There was little chance of Ty playing this year, but according to the doctor's current reports, he would have next season, and all the following seasons. His son, however, wasn't ready to settle for that.

Thank God for the boy's perpetual optimism, Jake thought. Some days it was all either of them had to cling to. But even on the worst days, the hope in his son's eyes humbled Jake and made him realize how truly special Ty was. A fourteen-year-old man-child with the heart of a lion and the soul of a poet. The poet's soul he had inherited from his mother. As for the lion's heart, Jake would have said it was less courage and more just plain hardheadedness that he'd passed on to his son.

His light changed to green, but before his foot moved from the brake to the gas pedal, a forest green BMW with darkly tinted windows and dealer's tag still taped to the rear window zipped across the intersection in front of him.

"Damn," Jake repeated as he flipped a switch and the light atop his police cruiser flashed red and blue. He made his turn and whipped into traffic behind the vehicle.

Just what he needed this afternoon. Another new resident of Bayou Beltane paying more attention to talking on their cell phone than watching traffic signals. He knew that Plantation Estates, the year-old residential development, complete with an eighteen-hole golf course and clubhouse, had brought much-needed money into the community, but sometimes he wondered if the price for a richer tax base wasn't too high. And the speeding car was a case in point.

The driver, a woman from what he could see, wasn't even slowing down.

"All right, Miz Leadfoot," Jake said, and hit the siren.

A FIGHT! ANNABELLE Delacroix Rowland shoved a wave of dark hair back from her face and increased her speed. The mental image of her fifteen-year-old son rolling around in the dirt throwing—and receiving—punches kept playing in her head like a scene from *Rebel Without A Cause*. Not that Cade hadn't fit that image lately. She had tried to be understanding about his rebellious behavior considering the fact that he had lost a father, home and friends, all within the last four months, deciding that if he needed to blow off a little steam once in a while, she could deal with it. But fighting was more than blowing off steam. Obviously, she had given him too much leeway.

When Anton Pelletier, the high school principal, called to tell her about the situation, he said there were no serious injuries to either boy. What did that mean? His definition of serious might not be the same as hers. Were they talking bloody noses or something that might require stitches?

Don't assume the worst.

But she couldn't help herself. Cade was all she had, and she couldn't get to the school fast enough. Directly ahead, the traffic light at the old Covington road changed to yellow. Instinctively, her hands tightened on the steering wheel and her foot pressed harder on the accelerator. She shot through the intersection as the yellow light went red, so focused on reaching her destination that she didn't notice the flashing red-and-blue lights atop the police car coming up behind her a moment later.

But the siren got her attention.

"Oh, no," she groaned, steering her car to the side of the road. Even as she automatically reached for her purse and started digging for her license, she heard the officer's footsteps crunching gravel as he approached. *Great. Just great. What else can go wrong today?*

"Could I see your license, ma'am?" the officer asked. "And take it out of your wallet if you don't mind."

"Yes, sir. I'm sorry, Officer. I really didn't realize I was speeding."

"Yes, ma'am."

"I was on my way to pick up my—oh, here it is!" Wallet in hand, she turned...and blinked, unable to believe her own eyes. *"Jake?"*

"Anna—" The citation pad slid from his fingers and plopped to the ground. "Annabelle?"

Totally shocked, she stared at him. Of all the people she could have run into today, Jake Trahan was the last person she would have expected. She felt her blood pressure climbing and her heart racing. She never should have asked herself what else could go wrong.

"Jake, I had no idea...that is, I didn't expect..."

He bent down, retrieved the pad, then removed his sunglasses and leaned toward her, resting his arm against the door. From his equally stunned expression she could see he was as surprised as she was. "Annabelle," he whispered. "Is it really you? For a minute I thought I was seeing things. I never dreamed..." He shook his head as if he still weren't able to trust his own eyes. "Well, it's...it's great to see you. How've you been?"

"F-fine."

What a lie! The one man she had been hoping to avoid since she'd arrived in Louisiana almost two weeks ago, and here she was caught running a red light by him. Not that she had expected to avoid him forever, but she knew he had moved to Covington when he became sheriff, and she had hoped that would lessen her chances of encountering him. Of all days, this was the worst for her to run into Jake Trahan.

"I, uh, I know I was speeding, and you have to write me a ticket." She ran a hand through her thick dark hair, the sun highlighting shades of auburn. "But I desperately need to get to the high school. They called about Cade."

"That's your boy, right?"

"Yes, and—how did you know?"

"Somebody told me." He shrugged. "Can't even remember who at the moment. But you know how people around here love to pass around information about everybody else. And it doesn't make any difference if you live half a mile from the bayou or halfway across the country."

"Yes. I guess I had forgotten."

She hadn't forgotten. She'd never forget that the "people around here" were part of the reason she'd left all those years ago. Part of the reason she had lived a lie every day since then. Back then she had been young and confused. And trusting. But her father had known the people around here and how they gossiped. He'd been quick to remind her that it wouldn't do for a Delacroix to be talked about, any more than it would do for a Delacroix to marry below her class. Now she had returned, newly divorced, with a teenage son, and once again dependent on her father. She'd just bet information was being passed around. Tongues were probably wagging like crazy this very minute. Well, let them. She wasn't that frightened, insecure young girl anymore. At the moment she couldn't state with emphatic clarity exactly who she was, or what direction she wanted her life to take, but she was getting there.

"Did you say you were headed to the high school? I thought you lived in Florida."

Annabelle avoided meeting his gaze directly. "We've moved back. I—I know I'm probably acting like an overprotective mother, but the principal's office said Cade had been in a fight with another student right after the last class, and I was concerned."

"Was he hurt?"

"I don't think so, but I'm not sure."

Jake handed her license back. "Then you need to get moving. I'll follow you."

"No! I mean, that isn't necessary."

"No problem. Besides—" he smiled "—I'll feel better knowing you got there in one piece."

Before she could register another protest, he turned and walked back to his cruiser. Annabelle took a deep breath, started her car and pulled onto the road. Jake followed behind her.

What could she do? She couldn't prevent Jake from doing his job, but the last thing she wanted was for him to get involved in this incident. Not that she actually had any control over the situation. Truthfully, it was almost a relief to come face-to-face with him after dreading it as she had. As long as she stayed in Bayou Beltane their paths were bound to cross. She would just have to deal with it, the way she had learned to deal with all the changes in her life lately. Day to day, sometimes moment to moment.

When they arrived at the high school, Jake parked the cruiser beside her car and helped her out.

"You really didn't have to follow me," she insisted as she headed toward the front steps of the antiquated building. When she realized he intended to go inside with her, she stopped, her mind frantically searching for a plausible reason to dissuade him. "Thanks, Jake, really. I don't want to trouble you anymore. Besides, it's probably something minor."

"Probably, but—"

"I'm sure you've got better things to do. Like finish writing out my ticket."

He smiled. "Sorry about that, but they're numbered, you know. It's no trouble. Actually, I was on my way home for a quick bite then back to —"

"Oh, then I positively couldn't delay you."

"No problem. Anyway—" he tapped the brass badge on his shirt "—this kinda stuff is in the job description." As he put a hand on her elbow to guide her up the stairs, he realized she was trembling. "Hey, don't worry. I'm sure it's not as bad as you imagine."

He had no idea how bad she imagined the next few minutes could be.

Short of a natural disaster in the next two seconds, she didn't see any way to stop him from accompanying her. When he knocked on the principal's door, she barely heard it over the hammering of her heart.

"Come in." Anton Pelletier glanced up. "Sheriff?"

"Not anymore," Jake corrected him.

"I'm sorry. After two terms, I guess it's a habit."

"Not anymore?" Annabelle asked, eyeing his dark blue uniform.

"I stepped down as sheriff over four months ago," he told her. "Two months ago I took the job as chief of the Bayou Beltane police force."

"And lucky for us, too, I might add," said Pelletier.

"Thanks." Jake looked at the boy sitting across from Pelletier. He seemed appropriately impressed with the appearance of a police officer. "Anything requiring my attention, Anton?"

"Oh, no," Pelletier assured him. "But I appreciate you looking in."

Jake turned to Annabelle. "Guess I'll be seeing you."

"What?" she asked, realizing she was staring at him. "Oh, yes." She offered her hand.

Her slender hand disappeared completely in his, and it struck him that he had forgotten how delicate she was, how soft and delicate. He leaned toward her and in a lowered voice said, "What did I tell you? Your boy looks okay."

"Yes. Thanks, Jake."

"Anytime," he said, gazing into her eyes. "It's nice to have you home again." With a nod to Pelletier, he left, closing the door behind him.

As Jake exited the high school and walked to his cruiser, he remembered the feel of Annabelle's hand in his. Like holding a small, soft dove. How could he have forgotten?

Maybe because he had worked so hard to forget.

But did a man ever truly forget his first love? he wondered. Or that first sweet taste of real passion—even when that sweetness had later turned bitter.

ALL JAKE THOUGHT ABOUT as he drove back to the station was Annabelle. He had truly believed he'd put the past behind him, but seeing her again sparked old memories. Images of the two of them meeting in secret. The stolen kisses, urgent embraces. And the need. He had never known what it was to need another human being until he had loved sweet and lovely, seventeen-year-old Annabelle Delacroix. And she was just as beautiful now as the first day he realized he was in love with her, the first night they made love.

On the heels of the old memories came an unexpected flare of resentment he'd thought long dead. Resentment that she had dumped him for someone from the ''right'' side of the tracks. Someone with money and a name to match Delacroix. The pain of her betrayal had been so deep he couldn't bear the thought of seeing the woman he loved day after day with another man. Right after Philip Delacroix had informed him Annabelle was marrying Neal Rowland, Jake had left town and joined the marines.

He smiled to himself. He wondered what Philip Delacroix would think if he knew that the hateful words he'd spoken that night so long ago were at least partly responsible for Jake's success. That night the old man had called him trash, telling him he would never amount to anything. Then he'd told him Annabelle was engaged to Neal Rowland and didn't want anything to do with Jake. Delacroix showed him a note written in Annabelle's own hand, and told him if he ever tried to see her again, or cause trouble, his mother and two younger sisters would pay the price.

Until that moment Jake could honestly say he had never hated anyone before. But he hated Philip Delacroix, because he knew the threat wasn't an idle one.

Delacroix owned half the parish, had powerful friends and a reputation for getting rid of anyone who stood in his way.

As much as Jake loved Annabelle, he had hated her father.

He had left Bayou Beltane hurt and angry…and determined. Determined to prove Philip Delacroix wrong.

That night had definitely altered his life. It was the fuel for his struggle to go to college on the GI bill. He had even married on the rebound. And even though his wife, Alicia, had known she wasn't the love of his life, he had worked hard to be a good husband, and they had been happy until she died three years ago.

It had taken him a long time to finally forgive Annabelle. How could he blame her for wanting security? Yes, they had been in love, but they were both too young to realize that love wasn't always enough. She had been born to a life of wealth, and he had been unreasonable to expect her to throw away everything for a struggling mill worker fresh from high school who could only hope for a better life.

He pulled his car into his assigned space, killed the engine and got out. Still, he thought, he couldn't deny that Annabelle had haunted his memories for almost sixteen years, and now…

We've moved back.

Now he would have to deal with those memories and at the same time come face-to-face with the reality that she belonged to someone else. That he could never be a part of her life. In that respect, not much had changed in sixteen years. He was still a working stiff with little money. She was still rich and unobtainable. Since they now lived in the same town, the best he could hope for was being her friend.

The fact that he had thought "the best he could hope for", made him wonder just how safely tucked away the past really was. Of course, it would be difficult for him to see her happily married to another man. He would feel the same about anyone he had loved as much as he had loved Annabelle.

The trouble was, he had never loved anyone that much.

Jake's secretary, Miz Luella James, looked up as he came into the office. "I thought you were in Covington for the day, Chief."

"I have to transfer that federal prisoner to New Orleans."

"Wasn't Jackson supposed to do that?"

"He called me at home—said he was sick."

Miz Luella narrowed her eyes. "Hungover is more like it."

Jake wasn't in the mood to debate the merits of Detective Jackson Boudreaux, mainly because it would have been a short debate at best. In his opinion, Boudreaux had very little merit as a law enforcement officer or as a man, unless one listed laziness and a talent for being slippery. Since the day he took over the Bayou Beltane Police Department, Jake had suspected Jackson had his fingers in quite a few dirty pies, but so far he had no proof. The day he did was the day Jackson was gone, and Jake couldn't honestly say he would regret the loss.

"I'll drive the prisoner to New Orleans, then I'm headed back to pick up Ty." He started to walk into his office, then stopped and pulled his citation book out of his back pocket. "The top citation was never completed. Will you make a note—"

"One of those little hellions from Plantation Estates,

I'll bet. What did he do, outrun you in one of those expensive sports cars they all drive?''

"As a matter of fact, it was a former longtime resident."

"Oh, who?''

Too late, Jake realized his mistake. From the glint in Miz Luella's eyes, she was practically salivating over the possibility of a juicy tidbit of gossip. He considered not telling her, but it wouldn't make any difference. At least a dozen cars had passed while he was talking to Annabelle. He was surprised she didn't already know. The best he could hope for was to keep the trip to the school to himself. "Annabelle Delacroix. I mean, Rowland.''

"Annabelle? What for? Why, she's the sweetest little thing in the world. She's never been one to speed."

"She, uh…well, let's say she cut it a little too close going through a red light. It happens.'' He shrugged, hoping to minimize the situation. "Everybody gets distracted once in a while.'' He turned to walk into his office.

"Well, I guess so, poor thing. What with the divorce and having to move back home and everything, it's no wonder she was distracted."

Jake stopped. "What did you say?''

"Just that I feel sorry for Annabelle. She's such a sweet person, and—''

"Did you say divorce?''

"Oh, yes. I heard it was final last month. That's why she's back here.''

Jake stood in the doorway to his office, stunned at the news. No wonder Annabelle had sounded so stressed and acted so uptight when he saw her today. *Divorce.* The word kept bouncing around in his brain.

"Who's the second officer?" Miz Luella asked.

"What?"

"The second officer on the transfer. Who did you schedule? I have to keep the log up to date, you know. Especially when it's federal."

"Uh, Harrison," he answered.

"All right." She opened the log book and made a notation. "That's all I need to finish the paperwork."

"Yeah, okay. Then I guess you can go on home."

Miz Luella gave him a dubious look. "I suppose so, since it's five minutes until quitting time."

"Sorry. Guess I lost track of time."

"And it's no wonder. Between your job and taking care of Tyler, it's a miracle you haven't keeled over."

"I'm fine."

"Fine, my foot. You worry about that boy from sunup to sundown. Now, didn't the doctors tell you that the tumor was completely encapsulated." She proceeded to tick off the items on her fingers. "And that they got it all. And that the chemotherapy is just a precaution."

"Yes."

"I'm not foolish enough to think you'll stop worrying altogether, but sakes alive, you need to relax. If not for yourself, then for Tyler. Won't do him any good if you come down sick."

Miz Luella meant well, but she'd never had children, so she didn't understand that he *couldn't* relax. Ty was his whole life. The thought of losing him had shaken the foundation of Jake's world. He would relax when the doctors gave his son a clean bill of health.

Jake smiled at his good-hearted secretary. "You're right. I'll try to take it a little easier."

"Good," she said, satisfied. "Now, I'm going to

type in Harrison's name on the transfer papers, then I'm going home.''

"Thanks," Jake said and left her to it. Not two minutes later she laid the forms on his desk.

"Good night, Chief."

"Good night, Miz Luella." She gave him a wave as she walked out of the department offices and closed the door behind her, leaving Jake alone with his thoughts.

Thoughts of Annabelle.

Divorced. He couldn't believe it. From what he knew, she and Neal Rowland had a good marriage. Rowland was a successful stockbroker in Orlando and made a handsome living for his wife and son. He wondered what in the world had happened. Another woman, maybe?

Jake dismissed the idea as soon as it popped into his head. Why would any man want another woman when he had Annabelle? She was still the loveliest woman he had ever known. Maturity had only enhanced her natural beauty. And the idea of another man in the picture was ludicrous. It might have been years since they had been close, but he knew beyond a shadow of a doubt that she would never dishonor her marriage vows.

He sighed, reminding himself it was none of his business, and it had no bearing on his life one way or the other. So he unexpectedly ran into an old flame and she still piqued his interest? So what? A natural reaction. No big deal. It wasn't as if there could ever be anything between them. Whatever they'd had was gone. They were different people now. Besides…

Why was he trying to rationalize all these old feelings?

Old feelings?

He didn't have any old feelings for Annabelle, other than wishing her well. And even if he did, he didn't have time to think about anything or anyone but Ty. They were both free, but so what? That didn't mean they could pick up where they left off. No. Too many years. Too much had happened, he told himself.

But that didn't stop him from remembering the feel of her hand in his, or the softness in her voice when she thanked him. It didn't stop him from remembering that he had once loved her more than his life.

"I HATE THIS PLACE," Cade snapped as he followed his mother up the back steps of Belle Terre and onto the veranda. "I wanna go home."

Instead of going inside, Annabelle set her handbag down on one of the two bistro-style tables, and pulled out a chair. "Sit down, please."

Cade slung his backpack onto the veranda and plopped his long and lanky fifteen-year-old body into the chair. Sliding down until he was almost sitting on his backbone, he folded his arms across his chest and looked straight ahead.

Annabelle knew better than anyone that her son could be a stone wall when he chose, and for the most part that had been his choice since they had arrived in Bayou Beltane. Along with being sullen and moody.

She sat down in the other chair and took a deep breath. "We *are* home."

"Mom—"

"Listen to me, Cade. I know the divorce and this move haven't been easy on you. And if I could change things, I would. But I can't."

"But why do we have to live here? Everything is old. It's like living in a museum."

"What you call old, most people describe as Southern charm. Some people even consider us fortunate to be able to live here."

"Then they're crazy."

"Well, crazy or not, it will have to do until I—we—can decide what we want to do and where we want to live."

"It's not fair." He turned and looked her straight in the eye. "Every time I turn around, somebody's telling me, 'Don't touch that. Do you know General What's-his-name used that thingamajig in the Battle of Who-the-hell-cares?'"

"Cade! I know it's been rough on you. And I admit that your grandfather gets a little uptight when it comes to Belle Terre and the furnishings, but after all, it's been in our family—"

"Uptight? Mom, he's anal about it."

"He has a lot of demands on his time, and he likes things orderly."

"Thanks a lot. I gotta give up everything. Get the biggest shaft job of my life, and all you do is make excuses for that jerk."

"Andrew Cade Rowland! Don't you ever let me hear you say anything like that again. You may have good reason to be unhappy, but that doesn't give you the right to be rude. Do you understand me?"

Annabelle's voice hadn't risen, it never did. But her tone told Cade she meant business. He sat up a little straighter. "Yes, ma'am."

"And as for the incident today, you're lucky Principal Pelletier decided to let you off with a warning. I wouldn't count on his generosity a second time. I can't even imagine what your grandfather's going to say when he hears.''

"Jeez, you're not gonna tell him, are you? C'mon, Mom. It's none of his business. I'm sorry I called him a jerk. Just don't tell him. He'll give me another lecture on being a Delacroix.''

"Cade—''

"Mom, please, I'm begging you. Granddad doesn't like me. If you tell him, it'll just make everything worse.''

"Of course he likes you. Why would you even think such a thing?''

"'Cause nothing I do suits him. As far as he's concerned, I'm one big screwup.''

Annabelle gazed at her son and knew he was hurting. The incident today had started over a wisecrack and deteriorated into a scuffle, but the seed had been sown almost four months earlier when he had learned of the impending divorce. He was having a difficult time adjusting, and she didn't seem to be able to help him. The attempts she had made so far had been dismal failures. What made her truly sad was that before the divorce, she and Cade had always had a close relationship. At the moment they were doing well to maintain any communication. Keeping today's incident between them was little enough to ask, and at least it was something they shared.

Annabelle sighed and leaned back in the chair. "I won't mention the problem at school if you promise me there will be no more fights.''

"I didn't start it.''

"Cade…''

"Okay, okay. I promise.''

"Thank you. Now, please go upstairs and clean yourself up. And change your clothes before dinner."

Without another word, he picked up his backpack and went inside.

He was right, she thought, watching him disappear. It wasn't fair that he should have to give up his home and his friends. It wasn't fair that he had to start a new life in a new town, in a new school. At fifteen he should have nothing more serious on his mind than his studies, cars and girls. The teenage years were hard enough on any kid. Being hauled up by his roots and transplanted halfway across the country to live with a grandfather he previously saw maybe once or twice a year only made things worse. And Cade didn't even have the comfort of the only father he had ever known.

Even before the divorce was final, Neal had carefully extricated himself from Cade's life. With the move to Louisiana, the remaining ties had been severed. The last two years had been filled with bitter recriminations and strained silences. She had tried to protect Cade from the truth, but he'd known the marriage was crumbling. And like so many kids in the same situation, he had blamed himself. Neal's withdrawal, emotionally as well as physically, only made it worse.

Seeing Cade's wounded self-esteem had been Annabelle's wake-up call. She vowed that her son would not be doomed to suffer the same kind of insecurities she had suffered when her parents divorced. She couldn't change the past, but she could make Cade's and her future the best it could possibly be. Just what the future held, she wasn't certain.

Except that Jake couldn't be a part of it.

She still couldn't believe she'd spent almost sixteen years running from the past, telling herself she was safe, and now she was back in Bayou Beltane. Right back where it all began.

And so was Jake Trahan.

After all the years she'd spent trying to forget him, all the tears she'd shed when she failed, now they were in the same town, mere miles apart. If it wasn't so ironic, it would be laughable.

But Annabelle wasn't laughing. This changed everything.

Jake was the last person she'd expected to see when she'd glanced up to hand over her driver's license. Her heart had leapt to her throat and she'd almost gasped out loud. And mixed in with all the surprise was a tiny thrill at seeing him again. She couldn't help it. She'd never been able to help it where Jake was concerned. There were some things a woman never got over, and her first love—for Annabelle, her only love—was one of them.

Jake in Bayou Beltane. Jake living only a few miles away. How in the world was she going to deal with this bizarre twist of fate?

CHAPTER TWO

NOT THAT FATE HAD EVER been particularly kind. It had lulled her into a false sense of security. She thought she was safe. Thought the chance of running into Jake was one in a thousand. The last she'd heard about him, he'd been elected to his first term as sheriff, and he was married with a young son and living in Covington.

And that was that. She'd tucked him safely away in a corner of her heart.

But he wasn't forty miles away in a nice, convenient office. He was here. Safe? She wasn't safe. Her whole life had been turned upside down today. Never mind the divorce. Never mind the move or the questionable future. What was she going to do about Jake Trahan?

Why hadn't he stayed in Covington? she wondered. Why hadn't he run for reelection instead of stepping down? After all, a man like Jake would be a valuable asset to any police force.

Annabelle realized she was making a judgment she wasn't qualified to make. Jake had still been a teenager when she knew him, but his courage and integrity had definitely been there.

He had matured, of course. He was taller, his body well-toned and fit. And, if possible, he was better-looking. Time had transformed the smooth good looks of the nineteen-year-old boy she had known into the quiet strength of a handsome man. But his smile was the same.

"Jake," she whispered, the sound of his name evoking memories she had tried so hard to keep hidden away. Memories of his gentle touch, the way his smile made her feel as if her insides were melting.

What was she doing, taking a walk down memory lane? There was no future in that. Thinking about what might have been wouldn't do her any good. Seeing him today had been wonderful and painful because it reminded her of the biggest mistake she'd ever made in her life. She hadn't had enough faith in herself to hang on to the love they had once shared. If only she'd known Jake would be here, she...

Stop! This is getting you nowhere.

Besides, what difference would it have made if she'd known Jake was here? Where else could she have gone? She wanted nothing to do with the so-called friends she had made while married to Neal, and there was no reason to stay in Florida when her family, her roots were in Bayou Beltane.

Of course, money, or the lack of it, had played a part in her decision. Until the few stocks she owned were sold and her CDs cashed in, she would have very little money. And regardless, what else could she have done? She had never worked outside the home, never had her "own money." Oh, sure, she had helped many of her friends decorate their homes, but always for the enjoyment she received, never for money. She had an eye for design and color, and decorating was fun. In fact, with the exception of being Cade's mother, it was the one thing she could point to with pride. But she couldn't deposit design and color in her bank account.

She had to be practical now. She just didn't know where to start.

Maybe some college courses, she thought. She'd gone for a couple of semesters when Cade was little, but then he became involved with sports, and the seasons never seemed to end. Between basketball, baseball or soccer practices, games and often tournaments, plus his social schedule, she had abandoned furthering her education for carpooling, the PTA and being chair of the school carnival—forever, it seemed. And those years were spent not just doing for Cade. She had worked hard at making Neal proud of her, as well. She had become the perfect hostess, played a wicked game of tennis and always kept herself fashionably current. Not that she hadn't enjoyed everything she did for Cade, or trying to be a perfect wife for Neal. But somewhere along the way she had lost herself, and now she wasn't quite sure just who Annabelle Delacroix Rowland was.

No, she decided. There was no point going back to school when she had no idea what she wanted to do with the rest of her life. One thing she didn't want was to continue to live at Belle Terre indefinitely, despite her father's generosity. He had told her she was free to stay as long as she wanted. In fact, he had all but insisted she and Cade settle at Belle Terre. Since her return she'd tried a couple of times to tell him she didn't want to live there permanently, but she hadn't followed through. Truthfully, she had, as Cade would put it, wimped out. Despite all her newfound resolve to stand on her own feet, she had never been able to go against her father's wishes.

As a child she had been daddy's little girl, always eager to please him. When her mother left, she'd felt abandoned and became completely dependent on him. She had never refused anything he had asked of her. How could she? He had loved her and cared for her when her own mother walked out. For that alone, she owed him more than she could ever repay. Through the years when he had reminded her of her duty to the Delacroix name, guilt had quickly squelched any spark of rebellion. After all, as he frequently said, everything he did was for her own good, and because he cared so much for her.

Her father had been a big part of the mistakes she had made years ago, but not all. She hadn't resisted him in any way, but instead allowed him to make decisions that had affected her ever since. For years she had blamed him for everything, but with the help of a therapist, she had come to understand herself much better. She would never have chosen the recent upheaval in her life as the avenue to independence, but there it was, nonetheless. So in a way, coming back was not just about starting over, it was as if her life had been interrupted. She needed to put those earlier years in the proper perspective before she could move on. Her father had been a big part of her life then. Now she had to find a way to face him as an adult.

All of which was well and good, but seeing Jake had changed the complexion of things and posed a lot of questions. Not the least of which was why Jake had acted as if he were truly glad to see her. By all rights, he should have been mad as hell after the way she had treated him. She would have been if the situation was reversed. But Jake hadn't looked angry today. He'd just looked wonderful.

At that moment her father's black Lincoln Town car turned into the driveway. It braked to a stop and Philip

Delacroix got out, looking as neatly pressed as he had when he left the house that morning. He had most certainly known Jake was in Bayou Beltane and she intended to find out why he hadn't warned her.

"Hello, sugar," he said as he stepped onto the veranda. "How was your day?"

"Eventful. And yours?"

"Tolerable." He set his briefcase on the table. "You know," he began without acknowledging her answer to his question about her day, "I never realized how much I miss being chauffeured until it's my chauffeur's day off. I'm just so accustomed to conducting business, reading the *Wall Street Journal* and drinking coffee on the way to my office, I'm spoiled. Admittedly, I love my creature comforts."

"Daddy, I need to ask—"

"I spoke with Neal today. Actually, his attorney, but it amounts to the same thing."

"What about?" she asked, Jake momentarily forgotten.

"The settlement, of course."

"Daddy, I told you there was no settlement. I never asked for one."

"Yes, and I told you when you were going through the divorce proceedings how foolish you were. No skills, no education, no money. How in the world did you hope to make a go of it?"

"By getting a job."

"Well, thank heavens Neal knew you weren't cut out to be a businesswoman, because he has generously offered you fifty thousand dollars."

Annabelle couldn't believe it. "I can't take his money."

"Don't be ridiculous. Under the circumstances, he's

being very generous. Besides, it's your money, too. You didn't just sit around on your fanny the whole time you and Neal were married. You made him a wonderful home. If it helps, consider the money payment for housekeeping and laundry.''

Sometimes her father could be incredibly insensitive. ''He doesn't owe me anything, and I have no intention—''

''Well, the money is yours, nonetheless. I suggest you think about Cade's college education before you reject it. And speaking of Cade, where is he?''

The mention of her son's name reminded her of the flying trip to the principal's office and her encounter with Jake. ''Upstairs doing his homework. Daddy—''

''Excellent, excellent. I'm very proud of that boy's scholastic record. It's not easy to maintain straight A's all through junior high and into high school. And it will pay off when he's ready to go to college.''

''Yes, I'm proud of him, too. Daddy, why didn't you tell me that Jake Trahan was the chief of police and that he was living here again?''

Philip went very still, then his gaze narrowed. ''I should have known once he heard about your divorce it wouldn't take him long to come sniffing around here.''

''He didn't know I was in town, and I doubt he knows, or cares, about my divorce. Besides, he's happily married.''

Philip opened his mouth to say something, then changed his mind.

''The fact remains,'' she continued, ''that you should have told me, Daddy.''

''Well, I didn't think it was of any importance.''

''You didn't consider it of any importance that

sooner or later I was bound to run into him?'' she snapped. "You can't be serious. He lives here. I can't just ignore him."

Philip pointed his finger at her. "Don't raise your voice to me. And why can't you ignore him? There's certainly no reason for you to socialize with the man."

Annabelle rubbed her right temple where a headache was beginning to bloom. Her father's attitude toward Jake hadn't altered one iota in all these years. "I just can't pretend he doesn't exist." To herself she added, *I've done that for far too long.*

"Can't, or don't want to?"

She glanced up at the disapproving look on her father's face. "I can't believe you would even ask such a question."

"You're…well, you're malleable, Annabelle. While that can be an admirable quality in a woman, it can also be dangerous. I simply wanted to remind you of your position as my daughter now that you're living at Belle Terre. And as Cade's mother, of course," he said almost as an afterthought. "Jake Trahan is a ruffian. He always has been. He always will be. And while that may be a handy trait for enforcing the law, it's not one I admire."

"I'm well aware of my position, Daddy. And your opinion of Jake. It's just that I wasn't prepared to run into him."

"Was he rude to you? Because if he was —"

"He wasn't. Not that he didn't have good cause. By all rights he could have been extremely unpleasant."

"Don't be melodramatic. Where did you see him?"

Annabelle tensed, feeling as if she were back in school facing her father with a bad report card. "I ran a red light," she admitted.

"Really, Annabelle. A grown woman trying to beat a red light. Well—" he sighed, his voice dripping with annoyance "—I suppose I'll have to handle it."

"Please don't," she insisted, a little shocked she had refused so quickly, so firmly. She had never done that, and hoped he wouldn't be upset. But the thought of her father even attempting to use his influence to fix a traffic ticket made her wince. "It might cause problems, and I know the less contact you have with Jake, the better you like it. I'll pay the fine."

"Oh, for goodness' sake. You make it sound as though I detest the man. I don't give him that much thought."

She suspected that was perfectly true. She also suspected that if Philip Delacroix had his way, Jake would be on the opposite side of the planet. On more than one occasion over the years, she had wondered why he hadn't arranged that very thing, but she'd never had the nerve to ask.

"But you're right. It's probably more hassle than it's worth. Still, I'd rather you mailed the fine in to City Hall. The less contact you have with him, the better."

Her headache was getting worse by the second. "I have no plans to *contact* Jake. Why would I go looking for trouble?"

Philip smiled. "Good girl. Now, let's go inside. I could use a nice, relaxing drink, then a quiet dinner and turn in early."

Without waiting for her, Philip picked up his briefcase and walked into the house. Annabelle stared after him. *Good girl.* That's what she had always tried to be. A good and dutiful daughter in order not to shame her father, not to sully the Delacroix name. A good wife, partly out of love, partly out of guilt. And where had it gotten her? For all her hard work at being good, she had come full circle with questionable progress.

Vicious circles, she thought, following her father into the house. And she was sick and tired of them.

ANNABELLE GLANCED UP in time to see the disapproving look in her father's eyes as Cade approached the breakfast table wearing an oversized T-shirt with some sort of cartoon creature on the front and the word Taz in bright orange letters.

"Good morning, Cade," Philip said.

After a quick glance at his mother, Cade pulled out a chair and sat down. "Morning."

"Forgive me for not keeping up with your busy schedule, but are you interested in sports at all?"

Cade shot his mother a what-did-I-tell-you look. "Yes, sir."

"Of course, it's too late for football this season, but you could try out for the baseball team. If you're interested, of course."

"Daddy, Cade played second base all through junior high and was a starter for his high school team last year. I wrote you all about it, don't you remember?"

"Splendid," Philip said, ignoring the reminder. "You should have no trouble making the team here. If I'm not mistaken, tryouts are just around the corner."

"Next week...sir," Cade hastened to add.

"Perfect timing, wouldn't you say?" Philip adjusted his bow tie. "I played basketball when I was in school. It would be nice to see the Delacroix name on a roster again." He winked at Cade. "Girls always seem to go for athletes, if my aging memory serves me. You must let me know how the tryouts go when I get back from Baton Rouge."

"I didn't realize you were leaving so soon," Annabelle said, not at all unhappy at the prospect of Cade and her being on their own.

"Well, I've plenty to keep me busy there. The wheels of state government may turn slowly, but they do continue to turn. I'm catching a flight in a couple of hours."

"I was hoping to continue our discussion."

"Discussion?"

"About my future, about me getting a job. I thought I might talk to Joanna and—"

"Don't waste your breath. What makes you think that ungrateful wench—"

"Cade," Annabelle said, cutting off whatever else her father was about to say. "Where's your backpack? We need to leave here in five minutes if we're going to get you to school on time. Please get it now."

"But I'm hungry," he protested.

"Grab a granola bar. You can eat on the way."

As soon as he was out of earshot, Annabelle turned to Philip. "Daddy, I can understand that this...estrangement between you and Joanna is painful, but—"

"Estrangement? I don't care if I ever see her again."

"You don't mean that." Since her return he had refused to discuss what had happened between him and Joanna, but she couldn't believe it was irreconcilable.

"Don't I? Your sister is a spiteful, ungrateful woman interested only in her own selfish pursuits. She and her daughter both."

"I know you're upset, but please don't say things like that in front of Cade. He's fond of Joanna."

"The sooner he learns who to trust, the better off—"

"What's this?"

Annabelle and Philip looked up to find Cade standing at the entrance to the dining room, a rock or crystal of some kind in his hand.

"Wh-where did-did you get that?" Philip asked, color draining from his face.

"Left my social studies book on the porch last night. When I went to get it, this was stuck in the back door. Stuck clean into the wood like a knife." Cade shrugged. "Weird."

At that moment, Mae, one of the three servants at Belle Terre, came into the dining room carrying breakfast on a huge silver tray. The instant she saw the crystal she gasped, and the tray crashed to the floor.

"Mae!" Annabelle hurried over to her. "Oh, my goodness, let me help—"

"Someone came in the night," the maid said, her eyes filled with terror. She pointed to the crystal. "Left a sign."

"A sign? What on earth are you talking about?" Annabelle glanced up and got a good look at the thing in her son's hand. Then she, too, gasped.

Shaped like a cigar, it appeared to be a piece of quartzite two or three inches long. Both ends had been sharpened to lethal points. It gave Annabelle the shivers just to look at it.

"Cade, put that down before you hurt yourself," she told him, then turned to the maid. "Mae—Mae," she snapped. "Stop talking nonsense and help me clean up this mess."

"It's a warning, that's what it is."

"Stop that," Annabelle insisted, then more gently added, "Mae, please pull yourself together. Now, I want you to go get a broom, dustpan and a mop. Will you do that, please?"

Nodding, Mae backed out of the room.

"I've been gone so long I forgot that voodoo is still prevalent in some—" Annabelle glanced at her father. His face was ghastly white, his terrified gaze fixed on the object in Cade's hand.

"Take it away," he whispered. "Now!"

Before Cade could move, Philip shot up from his chair and yelled, "Get it out of here! Throw it in the bayou."

"Jeez," Cade said, walking out of the room with the crystal. "Chill."

Philip sat back down and mopped the perspiration from his face with a napkin. "Ridiculous...ridiculous nonsense."

"Of course it is, Daddy. Superstitious nonsense. I can't believe it upset you so much."

Philip shot her a hard look. "I'm not upset, I'm mad as hell. Do you realize someone came on this property and...and... This is the thanks I get for being a public servant. We could all have been murdered in our beds."

Annabelle had never seen her father so rattled. "Daddy, you can't be serious. You've always dismissed the local voodoo incidents as bunk."

Philip started to say something, then stopped. He took a deep breath, his color slowly returning to normal. "I still do." He managed a weak smile. "It's just...just that I hate the idea that someone was skulking around the house while we were all sleeping. I've resisted putting in an alarm system in Belle Terre, but perhaps the time has come to rethink that decision." He rose from the chair, adjusted his bow tie and buttoned his suit coat. "Well," he said, eyeing the food scattered across the dining room floor. "No breakfast this morning. Just as well. I seem to have lost my appetite, anyway.''

Annabelle watched her father walk out of the room, once again in control. So composed, in fact, that she could almost believe she had imagined the frightened man she had seen a few moments earlier. But it wasn't her imagination. He *had* been scared. Having never seen that side of her father before, she wasn't quite sure what to make of it. Maybe he was under too much stress. And he wasn't a young man anymore, she reminded herself. Because he kept himself in reasonably good shape, it was easy to forget that he was approaching eighty.

The last thing she wanted was to cause him any more stress, but when he returned from Baton Rouge she would have to make him understand her position. To begin with, he had been critical of Cade too often to suit her. She needed to make it clear that even though they were living in his house, Cade was her son and she would be responsible for disciplining him. And she *would* get a job, whether he approved or not.

JAKE'S PATROL CAR was parked at the school when Annabelle arrived that afternoon to pick up Cade, and for a moment she panicked. Had Cade gotten into more trouble? Was Jake face-to-face with him right now, questioning him? Her heart pounding like a drum in her ears, she hurried toward the steps, then stopped when she saw Jake coming out of the building, his arms full of books, a teenage boy at his side. Relief whispered through her entire body. He saw her and waved. The boy walked over with him.

"Annabelle," he said, "I'd like you to meet my son. Ty, this is Mrs. Rowland."

"Nice to meet you."

"Same here, Ty." So this was Jake's son. He didn't favor Jake a great deal until he smiled, then it was easy to see they were related.

"Rowland?" Ty said. "Do you have a son?"

"Yes, I do. He's a sophomore."

"Me, too. Only I got promoted a year."

Annabelle smiled. "You must be very bright." He shrugged.

Suddenly she glanced up to see Cade loping down the stairs toward them and knew she had to divert him. "Well, it really was nice meeting you, Ty. I hate to dash off—" she took a couple of steps toward her car "—but I see Cade coming, and I've got to get to the, uh, drugstore." It was a poor excuse, but the first one that popped into her head.

Jake frowned. "Hope nobody's sick."

"Uh, no." She took several more steps, hoping Cade would notice and change his direction, but he didn't. He was headed straight for them. "Not really. I just need to pick up a prescription for migraines before they close." Cade kept coming, and she saw no way to avoid introducing him to Jake and Ty.

"Hey, Mom," Cade said, coming to a halt between her and Jake. He eyed the chief of police. "What's up?"

"Cade, I, uh, I'd like you to meet an old friend of mine. I guess I should have introduced you yesterday. This is Jake Trahan and his son, Ty."

"Pleased to meet you, sir,"

"Cade."

"Second period English, right?" Ty asked. When Cade nodded, he said, "Thought I recognized you."

"Me, too. But I haven't seen you in class for a few days. You been sick or something?"

Annabelle saw a muscle jump along Jake's jaw as he exchanged looks with his son. Ty glanced away for a second, then back at Cade. "Yeah," he said. "I have to have chemotherapy one day a week, and for a couple of days after I'm always kinda tired. That's why I've been out. I just came by to get some books."

Annabelle's gaze flew to Jake's. The pain in his eyes was so deep, so raw it was almost tangible.

"Hey, man...I'm sorry," Cade told Ty. He pointed to the books. "Intense homework, huh?"

"No sh—," Jake shot his son a warning glance. "Kiddin'," Ty finished.

Trying to hide a grin, Cade said, "Hey, you can borrow my notes from English class if you want. Got 'em right here in my pack."

"Cool." Ty looked at Jake. "Okay if we hang out over by the cruiser?"

"Sure, go ahead."

"I'm so sorry, Jake" Annabelle said as soon as she was sure Ty couldn't hear her. "I didn't know. It isn't—"

"He's going to be fine. And that's not just pie-in-the-sky hopes of a father either. They found a pea-size tumor in Ty's brain, completely self-contained, and the doctors are ninety-nine percent sure they got it all. The chemo is only a precaution."

"Thank God."

"Yeah," Jake said, watching the boys talking. "He's amazing. At the moment his biggest worry is missing baseball season and losing his hair."

Annabelle, too, looked at the boys. Standing beside the car, they seemed to have connected without any of the macho defenses boys their age so often felt the need to display. She could see it in the way Cade smiled at something Ty said. He was more relaxed than she had seen him in weeks. Ty seemed equally as comfortable. Her son's first friend in a new school and she couldn't even encourage it. She glanced away.

"They've got their priorities, I guess. Not that I even pretend to understand how the mind of an adolescent male works."

"Not sure I do anymore." He shifted the weighty textbooks in his arms.

"I should let you go," she told him. "It looks like Ty was right about his assignments being 'intense.'"

Jake started walking toward his patrol car and Annabelle joined him. "I just spoke to Anton about getting a tutor for him. Ty's been holding his own, but this is the third week of six weeks of chemo. His doctors told us the third week would be the hardest." He nodded in the direction of the two boys. "They sure seem to be hitting it off."

"Yes."

Cade was an all-or-nothing kind of kid. When he made a friend, he was loyal, faithful to a fault. He had left behind lifelong friendships when they moved to Louisiana and she had been praying for some new friends to take their place.

But not this. Never in her wildest imagination had she expected her son and Jake's son to become friends. Cade spending time with Ty wasn't a good idea, but she wasn't sure if she could prevent it.

"Cade," she said. "We've got to go, and Chief Trahan and Ty have got their hands full."

"Literally," Jake agreed, as he opened the cruiser door and put the books in the back seat.

"Comin', Mom."

"I mean it, Cade." He had a tendency to keep talking, and she wanted this encounter to come to an end.

"Gimme a call and we'll go over that stuff," he was saying to Ty.

"Thanks. I was sweatin' biology."

"It's cool."

"*Now,* Cade."

"Okay, okay." He gave Ty a thumbs-up sign and followed Annabelle.

"What were you telling Ty about biology?" she asked as they headed for their car.

"That I made A's in it back ho— back in Orlando. It's not his fav, so we worked out a deal."

"What kind of deal?" she asked, some sixth sense warning her she probably wasn't going to like the answer.

"I'm gonna help him with his biology, and he's gonna show me how to really get around on the Net," he said, totally oblivious to the possible backlash of his "deal".

"Oh, Cade. I wish you'd check with me before you go committing your time. You've got your hands full trying to adjust to a new school."

"You said you wanted me to make new friends."

"Yes, but—"

"And Ty and I have a lot in common."

"For instance?" she asked.

"We both like baseball. We both hate geometry."

"Cade—"

"And we've both only got one parent."

She stopped. "What do you mean?"

"Ty's mom died about three years ago, and,

well…Dad's not with us anymore, so it's kinda like we fit, you know.''

Cade's words sliced through her heart like a knife. Jake was alone?

Somehow it had helped to think of him as happily married to a woman who loved and cared for him. And even though in the secret recesses of her heart she could admit her own selfish desire that perhaps he had loved her more, she still wanted his life to be filled with joy. It wasn't fair that he should lose twice at love.

Cade had no idea of the pain his words had stirred. And how could she tell him that the ''fit'' was more appropriate than he could imagine?

She looked at him walking beside her and thanked whatever lucky stars shone for her that his brown hair was still heavily streaked with blonde from the Florida sun. But what would happen when it faded and reverted to its natural color, brown like his father's? Would the resemblance be clearer? Maybe it was true that most people took things at face value. But Jake was a cop, trained to look deeper. Today, he hadn't seen what to her was so obvious, but what about tomorrow, or the next day?

When would he look at Cade and see himself? When would he recognize his own son?

CHAPTER THREE

"HEY, MOM," CADE CALLED from the kitchen. "Aunt Joanna's on the phone."

Annabelle strolled into the kitchen just as Cade said, "Not a whole lot. Met this kid named Ty Trahan today. He seems cool. Yeah, sure. That'd be great." He handed the phone to his mother. "Aunt Joanna said she'd take me to New Orleans. I've never even been to the French Quarter. Can I go?"

"We'll talk about it," she said, taking the phone. "Go finish your homework." He left grumbling.

"Sorry," Joanna said. "I should have mentioned taking him to the city to you first, but Toni and Brody have extended an open invitation to the family."

"It's okay. How are you?"

"Fine. Busy, as usual. How's Drew?" Both Annabelle and Joanna had been concerned about their brother, Drew, for some time.

"To be honest, we haven't seen that much of him since we've been back. He's got a big project going that takes up most of his time. He's up early and gone before Cade goes to school, and frequently he doesn't come home until late."

"Is he... How does he seem to you?"

"A little distant maybe, except with Cade. And...worried, I think. By your tone of voice, I take it you know what it's about."

"Yes and no. He won't talk to me, of course. You know, in our last conversation before you moved back, I mentioned that it seemed every time I saw him at a restaurant or at a bar association function he had a drink in his hand."

"Well, I'll admit the two nights he's had dinner with Cade and me, he did have several drinks, but he never got drunk." Annabelle had hoped to be able to talk to her brother and find out what seemed to be troubling him, but so far, he had skillfully avoided any kind of serious discussion.

"Maybe I'm seeing problems where there are none, but I think he really needs a friend right now, so hang in there."

"Oh, I will."

"Listen, I called to invite you to lunch tomorrow. Please say you'll come. We haven't had any time to visit since you got back, and I want us to talk."

"So do I," Annabelle agreed, recognizing her sister's invitation as a peace offering. Since the day Joanna had called to tell her she was leaving their father's law firm to work at their Uncle Charles's firm, Delacroix and Associates, their relationship had been strained. Each time they had spoken on the phone they had both avoided the issue. Truthfully, she loved Joanna and wanted to spend time with her, but more than anything she wanted to see if she could do something to help heal the rift between her sister and her father. "Does Rick's still have the best hamburgers in the state?"

"If you like grease."

Annabelle laughed. "Okay, I'll take the grease and you can have something healthy."

"I need to make it early. Eleven okay with you?"

"Fine."

"Got yourself a deal," Joanna said, then added, "I've missed you, Little Annie."

It wasn't like Joanna to be so sentimental, using Annabelle's childhood nickname. Maybe this was a sign that she was missing her family. Annabelle hoped so. This luncheon would be a good time for her to do whatever she could to bring their family together again.

"I've missed you, too. See you tomorrow."

ANNABELLE AND JOANNA had just ordered when Shelby unexpectedly showed up and stopped by their table.

"It's great to see you again," Annabelle said, giving her cousin a hug.

"You, too." Shelby patted Annabelle's shoulder. "I'm really sorry about the divorce."

"Thanks. Uh, why don't you join us?" she asked, more out of politeness than anything. Not that she didn't enjoy Shelby's company, but she did want to talk to Joanna alone.

"Well, I guess I could." She pulled out a chair and sat down. "So, how does Cade like school? It must have been tough on him, leaving all his friends."

"It was, but he's adjusting."

"He told me he met Ty Trahan yesterday," Joanna said. "Sounded like they hit it off."

"Oh, poor Ty," Shelby said. "That kid has really been through a lot the last few years, not to mention Jake."

"Yes. Ty told Cade his mother had passed away," Annabelle said, hoping Shelby would fill in the gaps about Jake's wife. It was childish, she knew, but she wanted to find out what kind of woman Jake had married.

"If I remember correctly, Alicia—"

"Alicia?"

"Jake's wife. From what I remember, she went to visit a sister living on a farm in a little town about fifty miles north of St. Louis. That was a few years back when they had all that awful flooding and the Mississippi looked like an ocean. Alicia and her sister were trapped in the farmhouse. They both died."

"I hadn't heard that," Joanna said. "Of course, that all happened before Nikki and I moved back here. And not having spent my high school years here, I don't even remember Jake all that well, much less the girl he married."

"She wasn't from around here. Actually, I think he met her right after he joined the service. Anyway, Jake was already sheriff when it happened." Shelby sighed. "And now for Ty to be diagnosed with a brain tumor..."

"Jake told me the doctors are positive they got it all," Annabelle said.

Shelby looked surprised. "I didn't know you knew Jake."

"Well, I...don't really know him," Annabelle lied. "I remembered him from high school"

"But he's a couple of years older than you, isn't he?"

Leave it to Shelby to question her like a witness, Annabelle thought. "I think he dropped out a year to help his family, then came back."

"Well, he's certainly made a name for himself in the parish. He's honest, diligent..." Shelby grinned.

"And he's not bad-looking. But then you probably noticed that."

"Matchmaking, Shelby?" Joanna arched an eyebrow. "You're as bad as Aunt Mary."

"By the way," Annabelle said, wanting desperately to change the subject, "congratulations. I understand you're engaged to a rancher from Texas."

Shelby's grin faded. "There seems to be some question about that. Travis and I...well, let's just say there are some things we need to negotiate before we book the church and order bridesmaid dresses."

"Speaking of negotiations, Shelby, did you get that Calhoun brief couriered to Brody?"

Shelby looked surprised. "Couriered?"

"I'm almost positive that's what Brody wanted. You know he's been working on that case for weeks. The trial starts in four days, so time is precious."

Shelby frowned. "No, I didn't send it out by courier. I intended to put it with some other stuff going to the New Orleans office tomorrow morning. You think I shouldn't wait?"

"I wouldn't."

Shelby thought for a moment, then looked at Annabelle apologetically. "I hate skipping out on lunch, but duty calls. We'll have plenty of time to visit."

"Sure," Annabelle said. "Call me, okay?"

"Positively." She rose from the table and started to walk away, then turned back. "Oh, Joanna, will you bring me a club sandwich when you come back to the office?" She dug into her purse.

"Of course. My treat."

Shelby smiled. "Thanks. See you later, cousins."

Annabelle watched Shelby hurry off, then glanced at

her sister, who was innocently tearing off a piece of a wheat roll. "That was pretty slick."

"What?"

"The way you got rid of Shelby."

Joanna put down her roll. "Underhanded, huh? I hated to do it. Shelby is such a sweetheart, but you and I would never have been able to speak freely with her here."

"It *was* underhanded, but you're right."

Joanna seemed to pause for a moment, then got right to the heart of the matter in her usual straightforward manner. "I guess you've noticed that I didn't call you until I knew Dad had returned to Baton Rouge."

"Yes."

"I know you were angry and upset the day I called to tell you I was going to work for Uncle Charles, and—"

"More upset than angry. I couldn't understand how you could hurt Daddy like that, particularly when you know that he and Uncle Charles have barely managed to remain civil to each other for as long as I can remember."

"I know, but this is the first opportunity I've had to explain my decision." She toyed with her water glass as if trying to decide what to say next. "Annabelle, things—people—have changed since you left Louisiana."

"What do you mean?"

"Dad has changed. He's older, of course, but...well, let's just say that when we were growing up, I knew he was a lawyer, then became a senator, but I never really *knew* anything about his business."

"Most kids don't ever understand exactly what their parents do for a living."

The waitress appeared with their food, and Joanna waited until she was gone to continue. "It's just that you see things differently as an adult."

"Of course you do, but that doesn't explain—"

"I didn't like some of the things I saw when I worked for Dad."

In the process of spreading mustard on her hamburger bun, Annabelle stopped and looked at her sister. "What *things?*"

"I can't tell you specifically because most of what I know is confidential. Dad turned part of his practice over to an associate when he was elected to the state senate, and since then, the profile of clients has...well, it's different from what I thought it was."

"Different good, or different bad?"

Joanna looked her sister right in the eye. "Bad."

"How bad?"

"Borderline illegal, and in some cases over the line."

Annabelle forgot about her hamburger. "You told Daddy all of this, right?"

"Yes."

"If you told him his associate was destroying his business, his reputation, then what did you argue about? He must have been grateful."

"Annabelle, you don't understand. We argued because he knew what was happening and did nothing about it."

"You must have been mistaken, Joanna. Daddy would never—"

"You don't know him. *I* didn't really know who Philip Delacroix was until I went to work for him."

"He's your father, that's who he is. You seem to have forgotten that minor detail."

"No. I haven't forgotten. I'll always love him because he is my father, but I don't—can't—respect him anymore."

Annabelle felt stunned, she had expected father and daughter had disagreed over how to handle a case, and since both were strong-willed, it had gone past the point of reconciliation. But this?

"Do you know what you're saying? You're saying our father is...what, a shady character? Unethical?"

"Annie, be realistic. Dad is a power broker and a manipulator. He lives to wheel and deal. All I'm saying is power is a demanding mistress, always greedy for more. And Dad is also incredibly selfish and ruthless."

While a part of her wanted to deny everything her sister said, Annabelle couldn't, because she'd had similar thoughts herself. But once they were voiced, those thoughts sounded so cold, so disloyal. A wave of guilt made her feel as if she had to defend her father. "It sounds to me as if you just don't agree with Daddy's style of business."

"That's putting it mildly."

"Joanna, you and Daddy have disagreed before. I still don't see why you had to go crying to Uncle Charles."

"That's not what happened."

"I'm still trying to figure out what *did* happen. And where does Drew stand in all of this?"

"With Dad, of course."

She wanted to believe Joanna was exaggerating the seriousness of the situation. Their father wasn't unethical. But even as the thought formed, she couldn't deny he was a master manipulator. So good, in fact, that years ago he had convinced her that telling a lie was the only way to protect the family. Despite the fact that she wasn't thoroughly convinced he deserved her loyalty, she had to protect her father. In a way, protecting him was protecting herself.

"I'm sorry, Joanna, but this all sounds like a case of you just not getting what you wanted. You and Daddy argued. You lost and he won."

"I'm sorry you can't—or won't—see this situation, see Dad, realistically."

"Did you expect me to accept everything you say at face value?"

"No. But I didn't expect you to defend him blindly. You're a grown woman, Annabelle. No more little Annie, apple of daddy's eye. I expected you to be reasonable. And have enough faith in *my* integrity to know I would never deliberately do anything to hurt Dad."

"I know what a stickler you are for doing things properly and by the book. It's an admirable quality. But what about loyalty? What about sticking by your family?"

"I love my family."

"Well, you have a poor way of showing it."

"As I said, you've been gone a long time. Things have changed."

Annabelle took her napkin from her lap and placed it beside her plate. "I think we're going to have to agree to disagree on this subject."

"I think you're right. At least for the time being."

They finished their lunch, trying to make polite conversation and failing miserably. By the time they said their goodbyes outside the restaurant and Joanna headed back to Delacroix and Associates, Annabelle was already angry at herself for the way she had spoken to her sister. She did have faith in Joanna's integrity; that's what was so disconcerting. While a part of her didn't want to believe that her father was selfish and ruthless, another part suspected she had known for years what Joanna had only recently discovered. And she had just defended him. She had been back in Bayou Beltane barely two weeks and already she had lapsed into old behavior patterns. Patterns she had spent two years in therapy trying to break. How could she fall back on those old weaknesses? She loved her father, but his influence could be suffocating. For her own good, and Cade's, she had to be strong. She couldn't let the past overwhelm her.

As she approached her car, she looked up and found Jake leaning against the hood, arms folded.

"Did you know you're illegally parked?" he asked.

The fates, Annabelle decided, were conspiring against her.

"I'm batting a thousand, aren't I? Or maybe I should say a double hitter since this is my second ticket in three days. At this rate my insurance is going to look like the national debt."

Jake grinned. "Actually, you won't be illegal for—" he glanced at his watch "—another five minutes." He pointed to the sign that stated No Parking between the hours of noon and 2:00 p.m. "Saw you coming out of Rick's and decided to tease you a little bit."

Annabelle smiled back. "I'd forgotten how much you love to tease me." The words were out before she realized how intimate they sounded.

"Yeah. Guess some old habits die harder than others."

Just that quick the world shrank to the few feet they occupied. Was it her imagination or did the air suddenly thicken and crackle with electricity? Jake was looking at her so strangely, she wondered if he felt it, too.

Jake knew he was staring at her, but he couldn't break away. Memories of the two of them laughing together over some long-forgotten joke tugged at him, drew him to her as surely as day draws to night. Part of him wanted to go with the attraction while another part hung on to a tattered piece of pride that refused to let him give in. He had an overwhelming urge to grab her and demand an answer to the question he hadn't been able to ask all those years ago.

Annabelle saw the flash of anger in his eyes and knew she was on shaky ground. Sooner or later he would ask, and she had to find a way to answer him without telling him the truth. But she was afraid. Afraid he would see too much.

"How's Ty?" she asked, hoping he wouldn't ask the question she saw in his eyes.

He studied her for another second or two, then said, "Actually, he's the real reason I was waiting to see you."

"Is something wrong?"

"No." He pushed away from her car and they both stepped onto the sidewalk. "Do you have a minute to talk?"

"I suppose…sure."

Jake indicated the huge black gum tree near her car and they walked beneath it's welcome shade. "I just wanted you to know how much I appreciate Cade offering to help Ty with his schoolwork. "

"It was his idea."

"And I'm going to thank him personally when he comes over this afternoon. I told Ty I would check in on them a couple of times."

"I can do that," she said quickly. A little too quickly, judging from the puzzled look on Jake's face. "You've got a police department to run. And I don't mind keeping tabs on the boys." The less time Jake spent with Cade, the better she would feel.

"You sure? I usually check in with Ty every few hours or so, especially on his days at home. No reason to bother you."

"It's no bother. Really."

"Ty's really pumped about Cade coming over. With his treatments and everything, he hasn't had time to make many new friends in the two months we've been here. It's been hard on him not having someone to hang out with."

"I know. The move from Florida was tough on Cade. He feels like he's had to give up everything."

Jake leaned against the tree's trunk. "Sorry to hear about you and Neal."

She glanced up. "I see the gossip mill grinds as efficiently as ever."

"Oh, yeah. The system still works better than any modem yet designed."

"Well, I'm afraid the system will be sadly disappointed in me. I'm not very newsworthy."

"Since when has that ever caused a kink in things?"

"Never."

They slipped into an uncomfortable silence.

This was asinine, Jake finally decided. It was ridiculous for them to pretend they hadn't known each other before, and he, for one, wasn't going to tiptoe around the subject anymore.

"How long are we supposed to go on pretending we never knew each other? Because I've got to tell you, it's not working for me."

Her heart rate shot into double time. "Jake, I—"

"We were kids, Annabelle." He turned those wonderful, soft eyes on her. Cade's eyes. "Too young to realize it was doomed from the beginning. I don't blame you." It was only a partial truth, but he wasn't prepared to deal with whole truths just yet.

"You could." And he would if he knew the real reason she had walked away from him, Annabel thought.

"What good would it do? Like I said, we were just kids playing at love. If you hadn't come to your senses, I probably would have sooner or later."

His words shouldn't have hurt so much, but they did. "You're...probably right."

"We live in the same town now. Our sons go to school together. We're going to see each other from time to time, and there's no reason we can't be friends."

"Friends?"

"Yeah. Think we can make that work?"

Friends with Jake. Could she do that? She might as well, because that's all they could ever be. And it was the most logical way for her to monitor his exposure to Cade, since their sons were obviously becoming friends. Yet logic couldn't account for the way her heart beat faster at the thought of seeing him more often. And logic had nothing to do with the way her body tingled with awareness whenever he was near. It was a gamble.

"I—I'd like that."

"Good." He pushed away from the tree. "Well... guess I'll see you around."

"See you."

Jake smiled, then turned and walked toward his patrol car...calling himself a fool and a liar every step of the way.

For a man who had once been elected sheriff of St. Tammany Parish on a reform and honesty-first platform, he had just lied through his teeth. He hadn't bluffed his way through such a touchy situation since his days on the Shreveport police force. And then he'd only had to face down a heroin addict with a gun.

Kids playing at love, he'd said. If she hadn't come to her senses, he would have sooner or later. He must be a better liar than he thought, because she bought it. She believed him, when he didn't believe himself. When he knew in his heart he had loved her totally, completely. When he knew he would never have come to his senses where she was concerned.

Friends with Annabelle. Was it even possible? It had better be, since it was his brilliant idea. The truth was, he hadn't even known what he intended to say when he started talking. The bid for friendship was almost as much of a surprise to him as it had been to her. But it didn't take a rocket scientist to understand the rationale behind his suggestion.

He wanted a reason to see her, speak to her without the past hanging over his head like an anvil ready to drop.

So, he convinced her they could be friends. Then why couldn't he convince himself? Maybe, possibly, because deep down he knew that friendship wouldn't be enough.

TOO RESTLESS AFTER her encounter with Jake to go back to Belle Terre until it was time to pick up Cade, Annabelle decided to browse through some of the antique shops she remembered from her last visit. She loved all styles of decorating, but antiques were by far her favorite. Even as a child she had enjoyed the old more than the new. There was something innately soothing about spending time with things of bygone eras and making them part of her life today. A bridge to the past. No. No more thinking about the past, she told herself as she entered a little shop one block up from the general store.

Annabelle meandered through the shop, stopping to look at a piece of china here or examine a sideboard there, until she found herself among some architectural salvage pieces. Another customer, a young woman with long, curly rust-colored hair, was checking out a stack of stained-glass windows, holding up first one, then another. A Federal mirror propped against a heavily carved mantel caught Annabelle's eye, but as she picked it up, she saw the reflection of the other customer shaking her head.

"Excuse me. I don't mean to intrude, but that's a reproduction," the woman said in a lowered voice.

Annabelle turned the mirror over. "You're right. Thank you."

"You're welcome." The young woman set aside the stained-glass windows she'd been considering and held up two trefoil windows that had probably once adorned a church but were now devoid of glass and in need of repair.

"Those are lovely," Annabelle commented.

"Yes. I've come back to these windows three times," the woman said. "The sad truth is, I'm in love with them, but for the life of me I can't decide how to use them."

"How about over a fireplace?"

"Without the glass?"

"Sure. I— Now I'm intruding."

"No, please. I'd like your opinion."

"Well..." Annabelle took one of the windows and held it up. "I could see this in the center of some picture frame paneling, painted the same color as the woodwork. Or stained for a real focal point."

"Sensational," the young woman whispered, as if visualizing Annabelle's description. "You've got a good eye." She turned and held out her hand. "I'm Katherine Beaufort."

"Annabelle Rowland. Nice to meet you."

"What's your opinion on those two rather tired Doric columns over there?" Katherine asked.

Recognizing a fellow lover of antiques, Annabelle replied, "Definite potential."

"They would need a big room, but in the right place they'd be smashing."

"If they're really bad on one side, you could cut off the damage. Sort of end up with two halves and—" Annabelle studied the columns for a moment "— mount them on either side of a dining room door, or in an entryway to give it some height."

Katherine smiled. "You're a decorator, right?"

"No."

"Own your own shop, then?"

"Nope. Just an antique lover."

"Well, as an antique dealer, I must say you have a real knack for design."

"Thanks. I've done a few things for friends. Nothing professional, of course, but I do love it."

"You should put your talent to work for you. I can name at least three firms in New Orleans that would snap you up in a heartbeat, even without experience. Good designers are born, not made, and— Oh, would

you listen to me." Katherine sounded apologetic.
"Here I am giving unsolicited advice to a perfect
stranger, when I'm sure you've got a lovely job you
enjoy. You must think I'm either very rude or crazy."

Annabelle smiled, thoroughly enjoying her new
acquaintance. Katherine Beaufort was obviously a
woman who had no trouble meeting people and Annabelle liked her instantly. "No, it's a pleasure to meet
someone who loves old things the way I do. I'm glad
I wandered in here today."

"Me, too. And you've sold me on these windows. I
can't wait to tell my partner about your suggestions.
We have a shop in New Orleans. The next time you're
in the city, I hope you stop by." Katherine handed her
a business card.

"Oh, I will."

"By the way, do you know of a nice motel nearby?"

"I'm not a good person to ask. I just moved back
to Bayou Beltane after being away a long time. But
there must be one."

"If so, it's a well-kept secret. I usually just drive
back to the city, and I don't like doing that at night.
What this town needs is a nice, clean bed-and-
breakfast," Katherine said, motioning for the shop
owner.

"Well, good luck with your windows," Annabelle
said.

"Thanks. I'm around here occasionally, picking up
things for the shop. Hope I see you again."

"Me, too."

Annabelle left the store smiling. Meeting Katherine
Beaufort had been an unexpected delight and left her
feeling better than she had in a long time.

Strange that a compliment from a perfect stranger

could bolster her confidence, but it had. For the first time since coming back to Bayou Beltane she felt a renewed surge of hope and determination. Things were looking up, she thought as she walked back to her car.

She drove down Lafayette Street, then turned north on Cypress toward the high school to pick up Cade. She hadn't been in this part of town since her return, and with a pang of bittersweet nostalgia, she noticed the old Portier house.

Built around the turn of the century, it was a splendid example of Victorian architecture, and Annabelle was saddened to see that it had fallen into a state of disrepair. As a child she had always loved the house because she thought it looked like a castle, with its rounded corners at the front, very much like turrets. And from her teenage years it held even sweeter memories. There was a giant oak tree in the front of the house, near the street, and where the trunk branched out was a knothole about the size of a fist and five or six inches deep.

Perfect for a secret mailbox.

That knothole had been a cache for messages sent by Jake and her about where and when they could meet. Messages and love notes. Without thinking, Annabelle turned and parked in front of the house.

Memories flowed over her like honey over warm bread. Memories of folded pieces of notebook paper that bore such sweet words. Words that gave her hope and joy. Words that filled her dreams.

Thought about you all through Algebra. No room in my head for numbers. Just you... Tonight?

I love you,

J

I dreamed about you last night. Every night. You're the sweetest girl in the world. I'm the luckiest guy.

Love you, love you,

J

Slowly the haze of memories faded, and she stared at the old house that had once been one of the grandest in town. Like the love she had thought she and Jake would share forever, it had fallen apart. Her heart ached to see the house now, with its sagging porch and missing shingles. But at least it could be repaired, unlike the love she still kept locked in her heart for Jake.

Reluctantly, she started her car, prepared to drive away when something Katherine Beaufort said came to mind.

What this town needs is a nice, clean bed-and-breakfast.

When Annabelle looked at the house again, she saw it not as it was, but as it had been. And it could be again. She couldn't turn back the clock where her love for Jake was concerned, but maybe, just maybe, she could make those memories a part of her future.

All at once her head was filled with a million questions and ideas. Was the house for sale? Maybe it was ready to be condemned. No, she decided, clutching at the dream building in her head. The house was like an aging model. It might be in need of a little paint and powder, but it still had good bones. How much could a project like this cost?

Damn. A major stumbling block. She should have known it was a crazy idea.

No. She decided not to defeat herself before she even got started. There was such a thing as a loan. That's what banks were for. And instead of liquidating her stocks, maybe they could be used as collateral. She was looking at a lot of hard work and time. But so what? Look what she'd have when she was finished.

A home of her own. And a business. Something for her and Cade that no one could take away.

CHAPTER FOUR

"WHAT'S GOING ON?" Cade asked as soon as he got into the car.

Annabelle knew she must be grinning from ear to ear.

"Plans," she said. "Big plans."

"What kinda plans?"

"You'll see."

"Mom—"

"Nope. I'll tell you all about it as soon as I've ironed out the details, but you're going to love it." She wasn't totally sure about the last part of her statement, particularly when he found out he was going to have a real hands-on part in her plan. Oh, well, a little manual labor wouldn't do either one of them any harm. She was so excited she could barely contain herself. This was going to work. She was going to make it work. And furthermore, she was going to do it on her own, without any help from her family.

"Well, in the meantime, just do me a favor, will ya?"

"What's that?" she asked as they drove to Ty's house.

"Lose that grin. It's goofy-looking."

She reached over and patted him on the cheek. "Sure thing, sweet pea."

Cade groaned and tried to ignore her.

Annabelle didn't care. It was only through sheer willpower that she was able to compose herself enough to comply with Cade's request to ''lose that grin'' before they saw Ty.

''Hi,'' he said when he opened the door and let them in.

''Hey,'' Cade greeted him.

Ty reached for a baseball cap resting on the end of the counter and settled it on his head, but not before Annabelle saw how much hair he had lost. ''Thanks for letting Cade come over, Miz Rowland.''

''Sure.'' The minute Annabelle looked at Ty, some of the jubilance about her future vanished, and she reminded herself how fortunate she was to have a healthy child. Even knowing Ty's prognosis was positive didn't prevent the stab of pain in her heart. She saw now why he could only attend school for a couple of days at a time. Today was obviously one of his rest days.

If possible, he appeared thinner than he had yesterday, and so tired—as if just the effort of opening the door were too much for him. Annabelle had to squelch the urge to put her arm around him and assure him everything would be all right.

''How 'bout some leftover pizza?'' Ty asked Cade.

''Yeah.''

''Why don't you guys wash your hands and I'll pop the pizza in the microwave for you,'' she offered, not wanting to even think of Ty expending more energy than necessary.

''You don't have to do that, Miz Rowland,'' Ty said, but he looked relieved.

''Are you kidding? Transforming cold pizza into microwave cuisine is one of the things I do best. And if you don't report me to the etiquette police, you can both wash your hands with that bar of soap I see sitting by the kitchen sink.''

"I washed mine just before y'all got here," Ty said.

Annabelle pointed to a bar stool beside the serving counter. "Then you sit," she told Ty. "And you wash," she directed her son.

"She's not joking about microwaving food," Cade said while lathering and rinsing his hands. "My mom can do a lot of stuff, but she's, you know, lame in the kitchen."

"I should have bought stock in McDonald's," she said, reaching into the refrigerator for the pizza. "I'd be a wealthy woman today."

"Plates are in that cupboard," Ty told her, pointing to the row of cabinets over her shoulder. She found one and placed the pizza on it.

"Mom's limit is grilled cheese sandwiches, steamed veggies and tuna casserole," Cade teased.

Both boys made a gagging noise.

"Everybody's a critic. Besides, I make wonderful salads and fruit platters."

"Diet food," Cade put in, drying his hands.

"And—" she popped the pizza into the microwave she spotted at one end of the counter and programmed it for one minute "—don't forget great milk shakes."

"Hey, yeah. She's wicked with a blender."

She shrugged. "So, I'm not Julia Child."

"My dad's the cook around here," Ty said.

"Is he?" For a moment or two, her compassion for Jake's son made her forget she probably shouldn't even be here. She reminded herself that her goal was to prevent Cade from becoming too close to Ty, and here she was playing den mother. But she was just begin-

ning to realize how hard it would be to discourage
Cade, when she was having enough trouble staying de-
tached herself.

"He couldn't even make pancakes when my mom
died, but he's pretty good now."

"My dad was great cooking on our grill," Cade said,
obviously feeling a need to defend Neal's prowess with
a spatula. "Best hamburgers ever."

The microwave timer dinged, and Annabelle removed the pizza. "Ty, I didn't see any soft drinks in
the fridge, so if you'll tell me where you keep them…"

"I don't drink 'em much anymore because I'm supposed to drink a lot of water, but Cade can have one.
Whatdaya want?" he asked.

"A Coke, if you've got one."

"Should be some on the screened-in porch, Miz
Rowland."

Annabelle handed Cade the plate of food. "You
want to eat in here?"

"All ready got my books spread out on the dining
room table," Ty said. "Wanna go in there?" he asked
Cade.

"Cool. Let's go."

Annabelle watched as Ty slowly slid off the bar stool
and led Cade into the dining room. "I'll bring the
drinks," she called after them. A few moments later as
she was pouring the Coke over ice, she heard Cade ask
Ty how many more chemotherapy treatments he had
to take.

"One a week. Three more weeks."

"Does it hurt?"

"Nah. See this?"

She glanced over her shoulder to see Ty pull his shirt
collar back.

"It's a Mediport. They put it in to do the chemo so they don't have to stick me in the arm every time."

"It's under your skin."

"Yeah, but it doesn't hurt."

"Really? Does it take a long time, you know, for the stuff to go through your veins?"

"Yeah, but they got cable in the hospital."

"You go by yourself?"

"My dad usually goes with me. Sometimes he can't stay because of his job."

"Well...if you want, the next time he can't stay, I could maybe go with you." Cade paused, took a breath. "You know, just hang out and stuff."

"Fine by me, but there's not much to do. Gets kinda boring."

"That's okay." Cade shrugged. "I don't mind."

Annabelle stared at the boys, their image watery as tears slid down her cheeks. She had never been more proud of her son than at this minute. It took all she had not to run into the room and throw her arms around his neck and tell him so. Drying her eyes, she took a deep breath to calm herself, then went into the dining room. She set a tall glass of ice water in front of Ty and handed Cade his drink.

Ty gazed up at her. "Thanks, Miz Rowland. For fixing the pizza and for letting Cade come over."

She smiled. "Don't mention it." He smiled back and he looked so like Jake that her heart swelled. She was going to become weepy again if she didn't get out of here quick. "I, uh...I need to run a couple of errands, then I'll be back. Say, in an hour?"

"Okay."

"Yeah, we can blow past biology in that time. See ya, Mom."

As she left the room, Annabelle heard Ty say, "Your mom's cool."

"She's okay," her son replied with typical nonchalance. "Man, you missed an awesome dissection in class today."

As she closed the door and walked to her car, the realization of how quickly Ty and Cade had befriended each other hit her. They seemed totally comfortable with each other. Even though Cade was relatively outgoing, he had never been one to just jump into friendships, choosing instead to take the slow and easy approach. There was none of that with Ty, and the bittersweet joy of it touched her deeply and worried her at the same time.

And Ty. Sweet, brave Ty. No child of fourteen, or any age for that matter, should have to deal with chemotherapy and Mediports. Her heart had gone out to him today, and she couldn't help but think that if circumstances had been different, he might have been hers, as well.

AFTER STOPS AT THE BANK and post office, Annabelle went to the market to pick up a few groceries. Belle Terre's pantry was noticeably empty of the kind of items that appealed to a fifteen-year-old boy. Cade wasn't big on junk food, but she was relatively certain the cook, André Arcenaux, was not accustomed to stocking frozen corn dogs, vast quantities of chocolate syrup, Popsicles and cereal. By the time she pulled into the Trahan driveway, almost an hour and a half had passed and...

Jake was home.

She reached into her purse and pulled out her lipstick and comb before she realized what she was doing. She and Jake were friends, right? Friends didn't need to get dolled up for friends, right? So why the urge to check her makeup and hairdo?

"Oh, this is silly. Just get Cade and go," she chided herself, getting out of her car and walking to the door. She knocked twice and Jake answered.

"There you are. I've been wondering if I needed to put out an APB."

"I'm not that late, am I?"

"No. C'mon in. The guys are just messing with one of Ty's new programs. Want a cup of coffee?"

"No, thanks. I've just come from the grocery store and I've got frozen food, so I can't stay long."

"They breezed through the biology and went straight to the computer."

"Cade's been dying to learn how to surf the Net, whatever that means."

Jake laughed. "In our day, surfing was only done in a bathing suit."

"I don't even know how to turn on a computer, much less 'surf.'"

"Well, I'm afraid I've really indulged Ty since he's been sick. If they make it for a computer, we've got it."

Cade rushed into the room. "Hey, Mom. You got to see this. It is so *cool*. Ty's on the Web phone. He's talking to some guy in China!"

Annabelle glanced at Jake and he nodded. "China, Australia, England, Ireland. He talks to people all over the world."

"Mom, we got to get this!" Then he turned and dashed back into the other room.

"Uh-oh. I think we may have created a monster," Jake said.

"Oh, no, this Frankenstein was well on his way before today. Cade's got a computer, but he's been bugging me almost daily about this stuff, and I must confess, part of my hesitation is that I don't have the vaguest idea what he's talking about. The mother in me simply can't give permission for something I don't understand."

"You're welcome to take the Trahan free seminar anytime."

"Thanks, but I think Ty has enough to deal with."

"Then I'll teach you."

The idea of spending hours sitting next to Jake had a certain appeal, but it was also dangerous. "Oh... well...I don't know. The information superhighway has gotten along without me this long, why add to the traffic?"

"You never can tell when it'll come in handy. These days every business is run by computers. And they've practically doubled the effectiveness of law enforcement."

At the mention of business, her enthusiasm to turn the Portier house into a bed-and-breakfast came back full force. Since Jake was a member of the community, he would probably be a good person to use as a sounding board for her idea. He had just purchased a home here recently and would have a working knowledge of real estate values. At least, that's how she tried to justify bringing up the subject. In truth, she simply wanted to share her idea with him, crazy as that might seem.

"Speaking of business, someone made the comment today that what Bayou Beltane needs is a nice, clean bed-and-breakfast."

Jake arched an eyebrow. "Not a bad idea. The old

hotel closed down a couple of years ago, and the closest accommodations are in Covington or Slidell."

"That's what this person said. What do you think?"

"Could be a profitable venture if you had the right location, right house. Most of the B and Bs I've heard of, the owners live in part of the house and rent the rest out."

She nodded. "But do you think one here could be profitable?"

Jake poured himself a cup of coffee, took a sip and smiled. "You sound as if this is a project you've already committed to, at least in your head. Right?"

Annabelle swallowed the lump of fear in her throat at the thought of admitting it out loud. "Yes," she said. "The idea came to me this afternoon, and I think I can do it if the house isn't too costly, and if I can get a loan from the bank, and if—"

"Whoa. That's a lot of ifs."

Suddenly she realized it *was* a lot of ifs. And there were probably dozens more. Fear gnawed at her resolve and her enthusiasm flagged. "You're right. It's probably an impossible idea. I don't know what I was thinking of."

"I didn't say—"

"I mean, it would take Lord knows how long just to make the place livable for Cade and me, much less guests. We could be talking major renovations and repairs."

"I didn't mean—"

"Just because I think it would be worthwhile doesn't mean the bank would agree. I'd have to have a lot of capital just to keep me going until I could break even."

"Annabelle."

"What?"

"I didn't mean for you to think I'm against your idea. Far from it. I think it's great."

"You do?"

"Yeah. You and Cade would have a home and you could make a living, as well. Sounds workable to me. Sure, it'll take some time and money, but you can do some of the work yourself if you're handy."

"I could. I am. I love refinishing and restoring old things. And I...I have a little skill at decorating. And..."

"And?"

"I want to make this work, Jake. I really do."

He lifted his mug. "I can see that. Do you have a particular piece of property in mind?"

"Yes. The Portier house."

The mug never made it to his mouth. He stared at her over the rim of his cup for a second, then lowered it. "The Portier house?"

"It seems to be abandoned."

"I know." He knew because he drove past the house occasionally to make sure it hadn't been vandalized. Or that's what he told himself. Of course, that excuse didn't account for the couple of times he had inspected the grounds, particularly the giant oak.

"Do you know if it's for sale?"

"Probably."

Annabelle's heart leapt. "I...it's such a grand old place. I hate to see it just sitting there empty."

Jake nodded. "There's quite a few like that in Bayou Beltane these days."

"But this one is so..." She stopped herself from saying "special." "It's so unique with the turret rooms at the front of the house. And it's certainly big enough. If I remember, the Portiers had at least six children."

"Seven."

"That means there will be plenty of bedrooms."

"What does your father think of your idea?"

Annabelle saw the unspoken question in his eyes. What he meant was, did her father approve? In a way he was asking if she still *needed* her father's approval. Or had she finally grown up. "You're the first person I've told," she said straight out. "I haven't even told Cade yet."

Her statement shouldn't have made him feel ten feet tall, but it did. He knew he shouldn't put so much hope in the fact that she had shared her idea with him first, but he did. This very afternoon he'd told her there was no reason they couldn't be friends, and it was true. As far as it went. But if he was honest with himself, he was hoping for more than friendship. He didn't delude himself that they could ever go back and have what they once had, but maybe this time it could be better.

At that moment Cade raced back into the room. "Did you ask her?"

Jake was staring at Annabelle so intently it took him a minute to realize the boy was talking to him. "What?"

"Did she say yes?"

"Yes to what?"

Jake cleared his throat and set his mug on the counter. "Oh, yeah. I told Cade it was okay for him to have supper with us, if it was all right with you."

"Oh, I don't—"

"Oh, Mom, don't say no. We just got started, and there's gobs of stuff to check out."

"I would have to come back into town—"

"We can solve that," Jake said. "Why don't you stay, as well?"

Cade's eyes lit up. "Hey, yeah."

"No, I can't. I've got a back seat full of groceries that are already well on their way to spoiling."

"No problem. We've got an extra freezer on the screened-in porch. We can stick them in there until you're ready to go home."

Annabelle looked from Jake to Cade and couldn't come up with a plausible excuse not to stay, except that the thought of having dinner in Jake's house sounded way too cozy.

"If you decide to stay, we can discuss your idea some more. See if we can't come up with a plan of action."

She shouldn't. She knew she was treading dangerous ground. But how could she say no? Especially, she realized, when she didn't want to.

SHE WAS RIGHT. Having dinner with Jake and the boys was entirely too cozy. But, oh, how enjoyable. Much too enjoyable.

Jake proved to be an excellent cook, preparing spaghetti and garlic bread as if his ancestry were Italian rather than Irish. Her contribution was a green salad and a can of cold fruit salad, drained and mixed with some whipped cream. The meal was no threat to even mediocre French Quarter cuisine, but they enjoyed the food and conversation. Afterward the boys went back to the computer, leaving Jake and Annabelle to clean up.

"You don't have to help," he told her as she tied an apron around her waist.

"It's the least I can do." She glanced into the room where the boys were huddled around the computer.

"But I do think I should take Cade out of here fairly soon. Ty looks like he's tiring."

"He is, but I've learned that he knows his limitations better than I do. And I have to tell you that I haven't seen him smile this much in weeks. Thanks."

"And I haven't seen Cade this excited about anything in weeks." She carried a stack of plates to the sink, which Jake had already started filling with soapy water. "So the thanks works both ways."

Rolling up his sleeves, Jake stepped up to the sink. "Now, about your venture—"

"I can wash those."

"Don't be silly. Ty and I take turns, and it's my turn to wash. But you can dry."

"Deal."

"Back to your venture. Did you look inside the Portier house today?"

"No." She tensed, hoping he wasn't about to tell her the place was in terrible shape on the inside. "What's it like?"

"It's not bad. The last time I really took a good look, a couple of the second floor windows in the back had been broken, but I called Bud Snider over at the real estate office, and by the next afternoon they'd been boarded up."

"Then it *is* for sale."

"Maybe. When Mrs. Portier died a few years back, she supposedly left the house to her daughter. But the daughter is some hotshot doctor with a fancy practice in California. She didn't really want the house."

As Jake handed her a glass to dry, she realized they had moved closer as they talked. They were now side by side, their hips almost touching. As if realizing the same thing, he stopped washing and gazed into her eyes.

Wonderful blue eyes, Jake thought. So dark and soft they looked like velvet. He couldn't believe she was in his house, standing next to him, helping clean up. The feeling of rightness wasn't lost on him. Nor was the realization that if things had turned out differently, they would be playing this scene as a long-married couple. And after making sure their boys were in for the night, they would be alone together. In their own room. Their own bed. The sudden rush of desire hit him like a slap in the face, snapping him out of his fantasy. Almost. She was still beside him, and she smelled so good. So...inviting.

"I, uh, I think they, sort of passed it around among the other brothers and sisters for a while, but none of them have ever made any attempt to live there."

"Oh." Annabelle was so close to him that she could feel the heat from his body. Move away, she told herself. It was the right thing to do. The sensible thing to do.

"How do women do that?" he asked before she had a chance to move.

She blinked. "Do what?"

"Stay smelling so good all day."

The abrupt change in subject threw her, and she made the mistake of turning toward him. "What do you—"

He leaned forward and breathed in her perfume. "I put on after-shave in the mornings and by noon I smell like the dusty interior of my patrol car. But women always smell good at the end of the day. How do you do that?"

"I...we...we cheat," she said, gazing into his green

eyes. "Most of us...most women carry fragrance in their purse so they can reapply it."

He smiled and she felt a tingle in the pit of her stomach. "I can just see me bringing an extra bottle of aftershave to the station. Wouldn't be able to live it down by the next century."

"I'm afraid tonight I smell more like garlic bread than gardenias."

He breathed in her fragrance again. "Nope. Sunshine and flowers. It's nice."

"Thanks."

They fell silent and just stared at each other.

He wanted to kiss her. Standing right here in his own kitchen, up to his elbows in suds and dirty dishes, he wanted to reacquaint himself with the taste of her, the feel of her in his arms. Would it be as good as he remembered? Or maybe better? He had no business thinking such thoughts, but there they were, and they were persistent. He would be moving way too fast, he knew. For both of them. But knowing that didn't lessen his desire to kiss her.

The thought crossed Annabelle's mind that he might kiss her. It should have been enough to shock her back to reality, but it wasn't. Mainly because she remembered how well he could kiss. How skillfully. And how much she had always enjoyed his kisses.

"Hey."

"What?" they both turned, speaking at the same time.

"Just thought I'd see if there was any more of that fruit stuff left," Cade said innocently.

"You've had enough," Annabelle said, quickly stepping back and untying the apron. "Besides, we've got to go. It's a school night."

Cade shrugged. "Okay." He went back in to get his backpack and to say goodbye to Ty.

Jake grabbed a towel from a nearby rack and dried his hands. "We didn't get around to talking about a plan of action for your B and B," he said, wishing she would stay longer.

"I...I really appreciate the offer, but I think I'd better talk to Bud Snider and the bank before I think about a plan."

"Probably right. You also might talk with your brother."

"Drew?"

"He's a lawyer and he's got a good head for business when he's not listening to your father. I'm...sorry. I didn't mean to criticize."

"That's okay. I suspect you're right, and I will talk to him. Thanks."

"Sure."

"And thanks for dinner. It was wonderful." He would never know how wonderful it was. To be with him again, even like this, was almost a dream come true. And if this kind of easy friendship was all she could ever have, she would be forever grateful. She folded the apron, placed it on the counter and reached for her purse.

"Don't go yet." Jake hadn't intended the words to come out sounding desperate, but they did.

Annabelle turned at the quiet demand.

"Not without your food."

"Oh." She smiled. "I forgot."

"I'll get it." He left and returned a few moments later carrying the grocery bag of frozen food.

"Cade, c'mon," she called, reaching for the sack.

"I'll walk you out."

"You don't have to."

"I know." He crossed to the door and opened it.

Ty and Cade came into the kitchen. "Thanks again, Miz Rowland," Ty said, then turned to Cade. "See ya."

"Yeah. See ya."

"Stay inside," Jake told his son. "It's cooler out here than I thought."

Cade ran ahead and jumped into the car while Jake and Annabelle strolled down the drive. Neither was in a hurry.

"We really appreciate the dinner," she said when they were standing beside the car.

He opened the back door and set the sack on the seat. "And we appreciate the company. Let me know how things go with the house."

"I will."

Jake opened her door, and as she got in, he said, "I'm glad you're back, Anna."

She gazed into his eyes for several seconds before replying, "So am I."

As she pulled out of his driveway seconds later, she realized how much she meant those parting words. When the divorce was final, she had resigned herself to returning to her hometown. Once she was here, that resignation slowly evolved into determination to make the best of her situation. But tonight... Tonight, for the first time, she could honestly say she was glad to be here. And Jake was the reason.

That realization was quickly followed by the thought that he might not be so glad she had returned if he knew the secret she had kept from him for so long. Annabelle glanced over at her son. And how would Cade react if he were to find out? Would he hate her?

How could she even think about planning a future for herself and Cade, knowing it could all disappear in a puff of smoke if the truth were ever revealed? But she, Neal and her father were the only ones who knew. Neal would never say anything. And if her father had desperately wanted the truth hidden sixteen years ago, he certainly didn't want it divulged now.

That left her.

There had never been any reason for her to think about confessing the truth...until now. But discovering Jake was living here *had* started her thinking along those lines. It was insane. Telling the truth now would only hurt Cade and Jake. Why would she even entertain such thoughts?

Because tonight she'd had a glimpse of what she had thrown away. Tonight, for just an instant, she'd allowed her heart to hope. And if she wasn't careful, that hope would be her downfall.

No. She couldn't allow that to happen. She had lived the lie for this long. If she had to go on living it for the rest of her life in order to protect Cade, she would. Tonight she had let need overrule her good sense. In the future, she would have to guard against Jake's potent effect on her.

CHAPTER FIVE

"WELL, HELLO, STRANGER," Annabelle said as she walked into the dining room, having dropped Cade at school.

"Hello, yourself." Dressed in tennis clothes, Drew Delacroix was polishing off the last of a stack of André's outstanding pancakes.

"I was beginning to think I would have to call your secretary and make an appointment if I ever wanted to see you." She selected a muffin and a bowl of fruit from a serving platter on the sideboard, then sat down beside him at the table.

"Got to keep the Delacroix coffers full, you know."

She reached over and tugged the collar of his shirt. "Since when did they start putting coffers on tennis courts?"

Drew smiled, and Annabelle thought how truly handsome her brother was. He'd been blessed, or cursed, depending on who one talked to, with the same good looks that marked all the Delacroix men. But Drew had something extra, something she had always considered special. He had the most expressive eyes of any man she'd ever known. Even as children she had always been able to look into Drew's eyes and know what he was feeling. They had always been close. Perhaps because he had been so sickly as a boy. Or maybe because it had been the two of them, the only son and heir and the plain, timid girl, who had been left behind when their mother divorced their father, taking only Joanna with her.

"Dear sister, don't you know that more business transactions are conducted on golf courses, tennis courts and ski slopes than in all the corporate boardrooms put together?"

"So these are your working clothes, huh?"

He shrugged. "Okay, so you nailed me. I've been working like a dog on this deal I just polished off and I decided I deserved a rousing game of tennis. To top it off, I'm playing against a middle-aged, overweight client who thinks he's Bjorn Borg." Drew rubbed his hands together. "You know how I love to win."

"Mighty sure of yourself."

His smile slipped a little. "Of course I am. I'm a Delacroix, aren't I? Heir to the empire. Keeper of the flame. And you, I understand, are the new mistress of Belle Terre."

Annabelle looked at him as if he were speaking a foreign language. "What?"

"The reception Dad is giving next month. I understand that as his dutiful daughter, you are to serve as his hostess. A new position, I believe, created especially for you."

"Reception? I know nothing about any reception. Are you sure—"

"Very sure. Dad's been planning this shindig for all his loyal supporters for a couple of months. And now with you back on the scene, he just installed you as hostess."

"And I don't suppose it ever occurred to him to ask me if I was interested in attending such a party, much less play hostess?"

Drew arched an eyebrow. "What's this? Insurrection in the ranks? When did you become a rebel with a cause?"

Annabelle pushed her half-eaten breakfast away, wadded her napkin into a ball and tossed it onto the table. "This isn't rebellion. It's common courtesy. Dad has got to learn that I'm not a child anymore, and he can't treat me like one."

Drew raised his glass of orange juice in salute. "Good luck."

"He doesn't treat you like a child."

"Of course he doesn't. After all, I'm the heir to the—"

"Knock it off, Drew. This cynicism of yours isn't very becoming."

"Sorry."

"I'll just call him and straighten everything out. Parties were never my thing, anyway. Lord knows, I put up with enough of them when Neal and I were together, but I don't have to now."

"By the way," Drew said, "we haven't had much chance to talk, but I want you to know I'm really sorry about you and Neal. He was never one of my favorite people, but I figured if he made you happy, then he was okay in my book. Of course, if I had known what a first-class jerk he really was, dumping you and Cade the way he has, I would have found some way to make his life miserable. I still might."

Annabelle had to smile. "Big brother to the rescue?"

"We can afford a hit man."

At that she laughed, which she knew was exactly the response he'd been aiming for. "Seriously," he said. "You're okay about this, aren't you, sis?"

"Yes."

"And Cade?"

"Not as much, but he's adjusting."

"Good. One of these Saturdays, I'll see if he's interested in learning tennis."

"He'd love it."

Drew glanced at his watch. "God, I'm late." Quickly, he got up from the table.

"But I wanted to talk to you."

"About what?"

"Business."

"You mean the law firm?"

"No. I'm thinking of starting my own business."

"Well, bully for you, little sister."

"Can't you stay a few minutes and talk? I'm not even sure where to start and you're good at—"

"Sugar, any other time and I'd give you hours, but I can't just blow this client off. It's too important." He reached for his racket, which was resting against a chair. "What kind of business are you considering?"

"A bed-and-breakfast. And don't call me sugar. You sound like Dad."

Drew stopped and looked at her. "Bed and breakfast? You mean like a hotel?"

"Yes."

"And you would live there?"

"Eventually."

"But Belle Terre is your home now. I know it's big and maybe a little too showy, but it *is* your home. Why would you want to leave?"

It had never occurred to her that Drew might care one way or the other if she stayed at Belle Terre, particularly since he spent a lot of time away on business trips for the family's law firm. But for a moment she thought she saw a flash of pain in his eyes.

"Because I want my own home. Something that belongs to Cade and me. This won't be just a way to earn money. I want it to be part of my life. That's why I thought you might—"

"I—I don't have time to discuss it now," he said, cutting her off.

"Well, maybe at dinner."

"I'm not sure if I'll be here." He grabbed the racket and stuck it under his arm. "Got to go." And he was out the door without another word.

If she didn't know better, she would think he was mad at her. For the life of her, Annabelle couldn't figure out why he'd suddenly become so abrupt. She decided to ask him straight out tonight at dinner—if he showed up. In the meantime, she had more important things to worry about.

ANNABELLE PULLED UP in front of the Portier house shortly before noon and waited, rather impatiently, for Bud Snider to arrive. And while she waited she started going over some figures in her mind. The Portier heirs were asking only thirty-five thousand for the house, but judging from the calls she made this morning to contractors, she might need another ten, or maybe even fifteen thousand, depending on the condition of the house. Fifty thousand dollars.

Precisely the sum Neal had insisted she accept. Guilt money for the way he had treated Cade. All she had to do was say yes.

She was tempted, sorely tempted, in fact, to use it. But she wouldn't. The reasons she had rejected it in the first place still existed. Besides, she wasn't going to knuckle under at the first sign of a bump in the road. She hadn't even applied for a loan yet, so there was no reason to panic. She could do this. She *would* do this.

Bud Snider honked as he parked his pickup truck behind her car and got out. "Hey there, Annabelle. Long time no see."

"Hello, Bud." She got out of her car and shook his hand. "How are you?"

"Surprised. Yessiree, you could have knocked me over with a feather when you told me you were interested in buying this old place. Not that it's that old," he hurried to assure her. "I mean, they don't build them like this anymore. Solid as a rock. Yessiree."

"Could we go inside?"

"Why, sure. Happy to oblige. Now, you need to remember this place has been vacant quite a while. Of course, we've had potential buyers from time to time, but no one has had the vision for it that you seem to have."

She knew she was too eager, and Bud would probably try to use that against her if they actually made a deal, but she couldn't help it.

"Here we are," Bud said as he unlocked the door and she stepped over the threshold and into the wide foyer.

If Annabelle had been excited before, she almost shouted with joy now. The old house had definitely suffered from neglect, but not abuse. And the neglect stemmed from the fact that the house had been vacant for several years. Otherwise, it looked to be in excellent shape. Annabelle sent a prayer of thanks heavenward. If the plumbing, foundation and exterior were in as good shape as the interior, her Grand Scheme, as Cade had dubbed it after she had told him everything, might be even more attainable than she had dared hope.

"Now, you just look to your heart's content," Bud told her. "Any questions you—" The ringing of his cellular phone interrupted. "Excuse me."

Annabelle had already walked through the arch of the opened double doors and stepped into the large parlor and library. The wall at the far end of the room was covered with floor-to-ceiling shelves and even a few odd books had been left behind. On an adjoining wall facing the turret window at that end of the house was a fireplace. The fireplace wall and the one with the shelves were completely paneled. The detail, all the way from the baseboards to the ten-inch crown molding, was absolutely stunning.

"Yoo-hoo, Annabelle," Bud called, finally finding her. "I hate to do this, but I've got to be at a closing in Covington in less than thirty minutes, so—"

"Oh, but I haven't even begun to see everything."

"Well, why don't I leave you the key." He dropped it into her hand. "You can bring it by the office when you're through."

"Thank you, Bud. I really appreciate it."

"Happy to oblige. Take your time, now. The more you see, the more you're just going to love this house."

She smiled as he gave her a jaunty wave and left. He had no idea his sales efforts were wasted on her. She was already in love with the house.

Glad to be alone, she lovingly stroked the wood paneling on the wall next to the fireplace, her fingers coasting along the edge of the exquisitely carved mantel. The wood was pitifully dry, but the beauty was still there, its luster waiting to be brought to life again with polish and a caring touch. Her touch. In her mind's eye she saw it refurbished with just the right pieces of furniture and rugs. Pictures on the walls. Windows gracefully draped with rich fabrics.

Annabelle was so enthralled in her fantasy that she hadn't thought to lock the door when Bud Snider left. Slowly, she backed up until she was standing in the arched doorway, which gave her a view of the entire room. She took one more step...and backed into something solid.

Terrified, she whirled, only to find herself in Jake's arms.

"J-Jake!"

"Did I scare you?"

"Y-yes."

"Sorry. I should have said something. Let you know I was here. But..."

"But what?" she asked, her voice still breathy from surprise.

"You looked so far away. Sort of dreamy."

"I guess I was." He smiled, and she went more than a little weak in the knees.

This was no memory. She was in his arms! Only now did she realize what pale imitations her memories actually were. They had no warmth, compared to the reality of being held in Jake's arms. She knew it was a mistake to stay. Every minute she lingered only made her more aware of how much she wanted to stay. Years ago he'd awakened a need in her. A need for passion, both the giving and receiving. As her body responded to him now, she realized he still had that power.

Jake gazed into her eyes and knew he should release her. Holding her only reminded him of the past. And just how much he still wanted her.

"Anna," he whispered.

No one but Jake called her Anna. And the sound of her name on his lips was like a caress, sweet, soft and so compelling. She gazed up at him and her lips parted. She didn't know if she rose on her toes or if he bent his head. All she knew was that in another heartbeat, at long last, she would know his kiss again. The instant his lips touched hers, nothing else mattered.

Jake's head was swimming with the taste and feel of her. She fit him perfectly, he thought, drawing her closer, deepening the kiss. But then, she always had. She simply fit him perfectly. His body, mind and heart. In every way, they had been so connected. With a stunning clarity he realized they still were. Maybe they always had been. He had never stopped thinking of her.

Just as he had never really stopped loving her.

The admission rocked him clear through to his soul. He put his hands on her shoulders and gently pulled away. "Anna..."

Oh, God, she thought, he was going to apologize for kissing her. How big a fool could she be? Not a day ago he had told her he thought they should be friends. He couldn't have made it any clearer. And even if he were interested in her that way, she knew it was a disaster in the making.

"I'm...I'm sorry, Jake." She quickly stepped back. "How embarrassing for you."

"Anna—"

"No." She held up a hand to stop him from saying something patronizing. "I don't know how... You were absolutely right when you said we should just be friends. That's all...all we can ever be."

Her words sliced through him. One minute he realized he still loved her, and the next she was dashing any hope he might have for that love. He felt as if he'd just had the rug jerked out from under him. Then he looked at her face, astonished to see fear in her eyes, and was ashamed. He should have known it was too soon to expect her to be able to handle this sudden rush of emotions. She had just come out of a divorce, she was probably still reeling from the emotional impact. Was it any wonder she didn't want anything but friendship? Was it any wonder she was a little frightened? Hell, he was more than a little frightened himself.

"Anna, I should be apologizing to you. I *am* apologizing. The only excuse I can offer is that, well…it's been a long time since I've held a woman in my arms and…" He ran a hand through his hair. "Oh, hell, Anna, can't we just say I'm a jerk and leave it at that?"

"You're not a jerk." She couldn't let him take the blame. After all, she had been just as involved in the kiss as he had. Oh, yes, she most definitely had been involved.

"Well, then I'm—" *scared* was the word that came to mind "—the next best thing. Listen, can't we just label this a case of bad judgment and go back to the way things were before? I give you my word, it won't happen again."

Despite the fact that she doubted they actually could go back, a part of her wanted desperately to give it a chance. "We could…try."

Jake smiled again, and instantly she felt better. Hopeful. "Good. I'll take that." He gazed around at the room, eager to change the subject before she had too much time to reconsider. "Are all the rooms in this good shape?"

"I don't know. This is as far as I've gotten."

"Well then, why don't we take a look and see what the rest of this place has to offer."

"All right."

He let her lead the way into the foyer, then upstairs, following her from room to room, listening while she made comments, offering his opinion only when she asked for it. As they moved through the rooms, gradually Annabelle began to relax.

When they were finished, he walked out with her, making sure the house was secure. "Thanks for all your help," she said when he handed her the key after locking the front door.

"Some help. All I did was agree with your observations. You've really approached this whole thing with a level head."

"Now all I have to do is find the money to buy the house, research the period to make sure the restoration is authentic, hire quality workers—in other words, give up my life for the next several months."

"Hey, that's nothing for a stepper like you."

"I'm glad you have confidence in me, because I'm not so sure." She gave an inward sigh of relief. Maybe they could go back to the way things were before the kiss. The thought gave her a measure of security, but it didn't make her happy. "I'll let you know *after* my trip to the bank."

"And when do you plan to do that?"

"This afternoon."

"By the way, what does Cade think of your idea?"

"We talked on the way home from your house last night, and I think he was totally shocked at first."

"And now?"

"He pronounced it the Grand Scheme and insisted on coming to see the house straight from school. I've tried to make him understand how much work will be involved, how much work he will have to contribute.

He thinks it's 'cool,' so I suppose that's his official stamp of approval. The one thing I know for sure is that he's thrilled at the idea of not living at Belle Terre. It's way too stuffy for his taste.''

''Sounds like he'll be motivated to help.''

''I'll take all I can get.''

''Well, my money's on you, Anna. Will you call me and let me know what happens with the bank?''

''Sure.'' He was still calling her Anna, and she wondered if he even realized he had slipped back into using it so easily. It was a small thing, but spoke of the intimacy they'd once shared. Try as they might, she didn't think they could ever completely forget about what had happened today. And that small, nagging voice questioned how much energy she was willing to put into forgetting.

Jake helped her into her car and watched her drive away, then checked in with Miz Luella.

''Don't forget you got to speak to the first-graders about safety this afternoon, Chief,'' she reminded him. ''And Ty called. Said to tell you that there's no Cocoa Puffs in the house.''

Jake laughed. ''All right. I'll stop at the market before I go home for lunch. Anything else?''

''Nope. Quiet as church around here.''

''You know where I'll be,'' he said, and ended the transmission.

Jake didn't leave immediately. He was glad to have a few moments alone to try and sort out his thoughts. One thing was crystal clear.

He was still in love with Annabelle.

He always had been. Even Alicia recognized it, though she never had a name or face to identify. He had worked hard at being a loving husband to her, but the entire time they were married a part of him had kept loving Anna. She was never out of his heart or mind. And all this time he thought he'd kept her and the love they'd shared safely tucked away in the past.

But it was alive. Here and now.

One touch of her lips had been all it took for him to realize how much she meant to him, how deep was the love he still felt for her. For the first time in longer than he cared to remember, a peace filled him. A kind of serenity and quiet joy he'd thought beyond his grasp. He loved Annabelle. Pure and simple.

And his feelings weren't one-sided. She had enjoyed that kiss every bit as much as he had. In fact, he was almost positive she had made the first move. She had certainly given him a signal. But then, in a flash, she had backed off. Clearly she wasn't ready for a heavy relationship. Understandable. With the divorce, the move, settling Cade and now this project, she would have all of her time committed. Was that deliberate? he wondered. Had she set things up so that there was no room in her life for anything or anyone else?

Jake had no idea why her marriage to Neal Rowland had gone sour, but he knew Anna was afraid to try again. The fear in her eyes had been unmistakable and real. So she was cautious—he could handle that.

What he couldn't handle was losing her for a second time.

But he didn't have his head in the clouds. He knew there were considerations other than his feelings. Ty, for one. Cade, for another. But the boys already liked each other. And Annabelle would be so good for Ty. She had the same kind of sensitivity he had inherited from his mother, and he responded to her as he had to no one since Alicia died.

And he thought he could be good for Cade. He'd already seen the way the boy had picked up on the bond between him and Ty, the way he watched them intently. And a couple of times Jake had seen a real longing in Cade's eyes.

All of these things were important. Jake didn't delude himself that wooing Annabelle, and making her child and his a part of that, would be easy. But the most important fact was him loving her, and her loving him. If they had that, the rest could work itself out.

He would court her. Flowers, candy, whatever it took. For however long it took. He would find a million and one ways to be near her. A million and one ways to remind her of how sweet their love had been. He would campaign for her love as he had once done for public office, honestly and determined to win.

And he expected resistance. But he would give her the time she needed to realize what he already knew. That they were meant to be together. And with enough time and love, he would overcome whatever fears she might have.

The only unknown in all of this was Philip Delacroix.

Sixteen years ago, Jake and Annabelle had allowed her father to intimidate them both. But they weren't scared kids anymore. Anna might still feel the weight of Philip's influence, but she wasn't under his thumb as she had been then. If Jake needed proof of her ability to stand on her own two feet, he had it in her determination to make the bed-and-breakfast work. He wasn't fool enough to think the old man would welcome him with open arms, but he had an advantage he hadn't had all those years ago. Jake had spent ten years on the Shreveport police force and he knew how to deal with vermin. And that's exactly how he thought of Philip Delacroix.

He had no intention of destroying Annabelle's faith in her father or her love for him, but neither did he intend to let Delacroix call the tune. Not this time.

Fate had given him a second chance, and Jake wasn't fool enough to make the same mistake twice.

ANNABELLE PARKED in front of the real estate office but didn't get out of her car immediately. She had to be logical now. Dreaming about the house was one thing, making it hers was something else. She'd submitted her loan applications. Now she had to deal with Bud Snider. He had already seen her eagerness. Now she would have to play the buyer's game and make him think that at least some of that eagerness had faded. She didn't intend to haggle like a fishwife over the price of the house, but neither did she intend to let her love for it cost her more than it should. This was business, and if she wanted to be a businesswoman, she would have to be able to compete in that arena.

A new wave of confidence washed over her. She felt good about her plans for the future. And now that her relationship with Jake was back on a more stable footing...

Stable? Was it really? She'd been anything but stable when he kissed her. The instant her lips met his, the world had spun away, leaving her suspended with only his mouth, his arms for support.

Not a bad place to be.

No. She had to stop those thoughts. She was looking down that dangerous road again, something she couldn't allow herself to do. She had enjoyed his kiss, and if things were different, she would want even more.

But things weren't different. She had to make sure Jake never found out that he was Cade's father. She had to protect her secret and her son. No matter what the personal cost to herself.

Annabelle shook off the disturbing thoughts and concentrated on her Grand Scheme. She got out of her car, squared her shoulders and took the first step toward her future.

CHAPTER SIX

TWO DAYS LATER, after filling out more forms than Annabelle knew existed in the known universe, she was trying to explain the paperwork to Cade as she drove him to Ty's for another biology session.

"So, when do we get to move in?" he asked.

"Haven't you been listening to a word I've said?"

"Sure, the bank is looking good. The construction guy thinks he can do it for okay money. And all we're waitin' for is some inspections and stuff. So, when do we get to move in?"

"Cade, I know you're excited about moving, but those inspections and stuff take weeks, maybe even months."

He groaned. "You mean we gotta live in the Mausoleum for months?"

Annabelle couldn't help but grin. "Belle Terre is not a mausoleum. It's a grand old Southern home. And don't forget, once we move, there'll be no more servants to prepare food or clean house. We're it, buddy."

"Yeah, yeah, I know. I'll have to clean bathrooms, mow the lawn and help in the kitchen. Mom, I know all that, and I still want to move. Can't we just do it faster?"

"Trust me, son. I'm working as fast as I can." And she was, partly because she was in as big a hurry as Cade, but also because from the minute she had told him about her plans for the house, he had changed. For the most part, gone were the surly responses and sulking. Not that he was a model child, by any means, but she could see that he was happier. The Grand Scheme, which had now become the Grand Endeavor, was every bit as important to him as it was to her. He had even solicited Ty's help through the computer. Together they had found some very useful information regarding homes built around the turn of the century in Louisiana. Even though the house wasn't hers yet, she felt as if it were, and she knew Cade did, too.

As she drew near the Trahan house, she noticed Jake's cruiser parked in the driveway. She hadn't seen or talked to him since...well, since he'd kissed her. Or she'd kissed him. She still wasn't sure which. Not that it mattered, she assured herself. They had parted on good terms and the friendship was intact.

She had intended to simply drop Cade off, but with Jake present, she changed her mind. The thought of Jake and Cade spending time in each other's company still bothered her. If she stayed, she could keep an eye on things.

Ty answered their knock on the back door, and Annabelle thought he looked upset.

"Hey, Miz Rowland," he said. "Y'all c'mon in. My dad's here, but he's getting ready to leave."

Annabelle stepped into the kitchen and stopped dead still. Wearing a bulletproof vest and holding a shotgun, Jake stood by the serving counter, talking on the phone. An open duffel bag at his feet revealed what looked like a change of clothes, boots and a jacket inside. Their eyes met and she knew immediately whatever was going on was related to his job.

"Hold on just a second," Jake said, and put his hand

over the receiver. "Anna, I hate to impose on you, but do you think you could keep an eye on Ty for me tonight?"

"Dad, I can take care of myself."

"We had an agreement, remember? Now, it's either Anna and Cade, if they're willing, or Mrs. Segal."

Ty rolled his eyes. "No contest."

"Anna?"

"Of course, he's welcome to stay with us."

Jake took his hand away. "Mrs. Segal, a friend of Ty's has just offered to watch out for him. She's got a boy near his age and ... yes ma'am, I'll be careful, and thanks again."

"What's going on?" Annabelle asked, almost afraid to hear the answer.

"An escaped prisoner from Angola. He's got family near Picayune, Mississippi, and the state police seem to think he'll come through this area. He's armed and supposedly familiar with the swamps and bayous all around here."

"Oh, my God. But that's so dangerous."

"It's my job, Anna."

Of course she knew he was chief of police, but for the first time she realized what that meant. Criminals, escaped convicts and God knew what else. They were his job. This was no traffic violation he was talking about, but a manhunt.

"It's routine, but you never know how long it'll take. I could be gone three hours or all night."

"Don't worry. We'll take Ty home with us."

He zipped the duffel bag closed. "Cade, would you carry this out to my car?"

"Sure. No problem," Cade said as he shouldered the bag and left.

Jake and Ty walked into the dining room. As Annabelle watched, she realized this was a ritual they had gone through before. How many times, she wondered, had they said farewell like this, Jake going off to do his job, Ty waiting for him to come back? When she saw them embrace, she turned away.

Jake walked back into the kitchen and picked up his hat. "Will you walk me to my car?"

"Of course." They stepped out onto the back porch just as Cade came in.

"All squared away, Mr., uh, Chief," he said, and went inside.

When the door closed behind him, Jake turned to Annabelle. "This may sound ungrateful, considering the fact that you've been kind enough to volunteer, but do you think it would be possible for you to stay here rather than take Ty to Belle Terre?"

Jake knew he was taking advantage of the situation, but he wanted her in his home with his son. There was something very comforting just knowing she was here. He also hoped it would strengthen the bond of his "friendship" with her. "He's one brave kid, but I think he'd feel more secure at home."

"If that's the way you want it, that's the way it will be." She was trying to be as brave as Ty, but she wasn't having much luck. All she could think about was that Jake could get hurt. Or worse.

"Thanks." He turned to leave.

"Jake?"

"Yeah."

"Be careful," she said. "Be very careful."

He smiled. "I always am." And then he was in his car and gone.

Annabelle stood on the porch and watched until his

car turned the corner and vanished from sight. *Dear Lord, please keep him safe. Please bring him back to me.*

ANNABELLE TRIED TO KEEP Ty's mind off the situation, but admittedly it was as much for her sake as his. Every time she thought about where Jake was and what he was doing, fear clutched at her heart. After the three of them prepared dinner, she had the boys do the dishes while she swept and mopped the floor. As long as they kept busy, they wouldn't have time to worry about Jake. She even got Ty to give her a very rudimentary lesson on the computer. Several times she considered turning on the radio or television, but decided against it for fear they might hear that the manhunt had turned violent. This was one night she would gladly miss the local six o'clock news.

As dusk dissolved into darkness, she called Belle Terre. Mae answered the phone, but thankfully, Drew was home. Annabelle could tell by his speech that he'd been drinking.

"Where the hell are you?" he demanded.

"Chief Trahan's house. His son and Cade are friends, and I promised Jake I would keep an eye on Ty until he gets back."

"Back from where?"

"A police call. Now, listen, Drew, I just wanted you to know Cade and I are all right, and that we might not be home until morning. Understand?"

"Guess so. Long as you're okay."

"We are. And, Drew?"

"Huh?"

"If Dad should call, just tell him we're with a friend of Cade's. But don't tell him who."

"If that's the way you want it."

"Thanks. And maybe you better get some sleep, okay?"

"'Kay."

Annabelle doubted her brother would even remember she'd called.

After she'd hung up, she managed to talk the boys into playing a game of Monopoly. They played for a couple of hours, until she and Ty lost all their money to Cade and had to declare bankruptcy. In an effort to keep things as normal as possible, she sent them to bed right after the game, with Cade in a sleeping bag on the floor of Ty's room. The only other bedroom was Jake's, so she opted for the sofa in the living room. But as soon as the boys were asleep, she got up, made a pot of coffee and prepared to wait.

And the waiting was torture. Where was he? Was he hurt? Was he alive? How did the husbands and wives of police officers stand it, day in and day out, year after year? she wondered.

Jake had assured her tonight was routine, but it wasn't routine to her. All she could think about was what would happen if he didn't come home? What if Ty was left alone? What if she never saw Jake again?

"Dear Lord, please bring him back to me."

Had she actually spoken those words? They must have come straight from her heart, bypassing the defenses she was trying so hard to maintain. For years she had denied loving him, except in her most secret thoughts and dreams. She'd gone through life pretending he didn't exist because she felt it was her only choice. Then two years ago Cade had been in a car accident and broken his leg. The doctors had thought at first a transfusion might be required, and that was when Neal had discovered the secret she'd kept from him since Cade was born. Cade's blood type didn't match his or hers. From that time on, her life had slowly disintegrated until, finally, the divorce and the move back to Louisiana.

And Jake.

She hadn't gone looking for him. He'd simply walked back into her life and nothing had been the same since. Loving him from a safe distance had been one thing. She'd even convinced herself that she could handle living in the same town with him. But the reality was something she'd never expected. She knew now that she had been kidding herself if she thought she could live the rest of her life in peaceful coexistence with the only man who had ever meant anything to her. The only man she would ever love.

Annabelle poured herself another cup of coffee and watched the minutes crawl by with the speed of an inchworm. Knowing she was only making herself crazy by staring at the clock, she took her coffee into the living room and curled up with a magazine. The caffeine worked until about 2:00 a.m., when she must have dozed off. Suddenly a noise startled her awake. Ty was standing in the doorway to the living room.

"He's not home yet?"

She shook her head. "I'm sorry."

He looked like an old man standing there in one of Jake's T-shirts, which all but swallowed him, wisps of hair sticking out from his head. Her heart ached for him and she longed to hold him, comfort him. But she hesitated, knowing teenage males were mercurial creatures. One minute they were like a small boy wanting his parent to kiss his hurt and make it better. The next, a man ready to face the world. At that moment, Ty looked caught between the two.

"He'll be all right," he said.

"Of course he will." But Annabelle didn't have nearly the confidence she saw in the boy's eyes. "I guess you've been through this before."

"Yeah. Some." He padded across the floor and sat down beside her on the sofa. "I can barely remember when he was a cop in Shreveport, but I know he had to go out like this lots of times. Not so much when he was sheriff. That's the only bad part about him being chief of police. He has to go on practically every call. But he says the good part is that there's not a lot of murder and, uh, may...may..."

"Mayhem?"

"Yeah, mayhem in a little town like Bayou Beltane."

It was the most Ty had ever spoken with her, and she knew it was partly due to nerves. "Thank goodness he's right about that."

"Would you please not mention I was up worrying about him? You see, we've got an agreement. Dad promises to take real good care of himself, and I promise not to worry, so I'd just as soon you didn't tell him."

"If you don't want me to."

Ty gazed up at her with soft brown eyes so full of concern it was all she could do not to put her arms around him. "I'm real glad you're here, Miz Rowland."

"So am I, Ty." She longed to offer a comforting touch and dared to put her hand on his. "So am I."

They sat like that for a long time, until finally Annabelle realized he had fallen asleep. Carefully, she slipped from the sofa, and holding his head and shoulders gently, she eased him down and pulled the blanket over his narrow shoulders. She took up her solitary vigil once more in a nearby chair.

It was about an hour later when she heard Jake's car slowly roll into the driveway. She glanced over at Ty, but he was sound asleep. Quietly, quickly, she made her way to the kitchen. She was halfway across the floor when she heard a soft tap on the door, then the welcome sound of his voice.

"Anna. It's—"

She raced to the door, jerking it open before he finished his sentence. "Are you all right? You're not hurt, are you?"

He stepped past her and dropped his duffel bag on the floor. "Good Lord, no I'm—"

"Oh, Jake," she whispered. "I was so...so worried about you."

She stood there, trembling like a leaf in the wind, tears running down her cheeks. Jake knew that what had happened tonight was completely out of her realm of experience. She wasn't used to the kinds of risks that were a part of his job. Despite the fact that he hated to see her so upset, he couldn't help but be glad that she'd been so worried about him. It was vain of him and more than a little bit selfish, but it meant she cared. It was the first real ray of hope she had given him, and he was trying not to press his advantage. That wouldn't be very gentlemanly, he told himself. It would be unfair. Maybe so, but he couldn't forget the way she'd felt in his arms the other day. The way she tasted, the softness of her skin.

Self-sacrifice be damned, he decided, and reached

for her. She came into his arms as naturally as though sixteen years had never passed.

"Anna, Anna. I'm sorry. I should have called."

She rested her head on his chest, grateful for the sound of his heartbeat beneath her ear. "You're here now. That's all that's important."

He held her tight, for the moment content simply with that. Heaven, he thought. Holding her was a little piece of heaven. When he finally drew back, he slipped his hand to the nape of her neck. "I think I'd better warn you. I'm about to go back on my word."

She should have protested. But how could she when his mouth was on hers, tender and demanding at the same time? And what could she say? That his kiss wasn't the very thing she craved? That it didn't make her feel treasured and desired? It would have been a lie.

Her body roused, humming with anticipation, as if it were waking from a long, dark sleep and taking that first dizzying step into the sunlight. She clutched at his shirt to bring him closer, urging him to take the kiss deeper.

He had expected hesitation, and when there was none, he gave in to his hunger, taking greedy possession of her mouth. This was the Anna of his dreams. His Anna. Memory swirled with reality. He felt complete, as if a part of himself, missing for so long, had suddenly returned.

Annabelle's head was spinning and so was she. Out of control. Dangerously out of control. The need she felt threatened to overwhelm her, and she fought the urge to succumb. Too risky, she reminded herself. Too much at stake. Not just herself, but...

"The boys," she said, finally able to snap back to reality. "What if one of them —"

"They're sound asleep."

He reached for her again, but she stepped back, knowing it was safer that way. The more distance, the better. "You can't be sure. Ty was awake earlier."

Jake could see the mood had been broken. He could also see that she would probably retreat as she had before. She was trying desperately to protect herself, and he wondered again if her ex-husband had done something to make her distrust her own emotions. The young woman he had known had been shy initially, but after the first taste of passion, she had become an ardent lover.

"This isn't a good idea, Jake."

"I disagree."

"We agreed to be friends."

"We were friends *and* lovers once."

She shook her head. "That was a long time ago. Too long. We can't go back."

"Who says I want to?"

"But you—"

"Kissed you. And you kissed me back. And I want you, and you want me right back. Don't deny it."

She couldn't. Lord, but it would make her life so much easier if she could. "Jake—"

"What are you so afraid of?"

"Afraid?" Panic skittered down her spine. "I'm not afraid of anything."

He caught the flash of fear and his gaze narrowed. "I've got no right to ask this, but I'm going to, anyway. Did Neal Rowland mistreat you?"

"No."

"Then what is it?" He took her hand and refused to

let her pull away. "It's me, Anna," he said softly. "You can tell me."

But she couldn't. Ever. "There's nothing to tell, Jake." She managed to pull her hand free. "I think maybe we've just gotten tangled up in some old memories."

"I wasn't tangled up in anything but your arms a moment ago. And I damn sure wasn't thinking about what we used to have. You want the truth? I was concentrating pretty heavily on what we could have— if you'd only give us a chance."

"There is no us, Jake." She turned to walk away. "I've got to get Cade up."

"Anna. Look at me." Slowly, she faced him. "Before you leave, you need to know two things. First, whatever you're running from can't be so terrible that I wouldn't understand. Believe me, if I've learned nothing else since losing my wife and almost losing my son, I've learned that life is too precious and too short to waste time judging other people. Second, I'm not going to give up on us." When she started to protest, he raised his hand. "I know. You said there is no us. But you're wrong. There is. There always has been. And I intend to do my best to make you believe that."

It was futile to argue when she couldn't offer the evidence needed to convince him that he was so utterly, totally wrong. Without another word, she left the room and went to wake Cade.

JAKE WAS SERIOUS. Dead serious, she thought as she drove toward Belle Terre with Cade asleep in the back seat. If he said he was going to make her believe in the two of them, then she was in trouble. He had been the most determined boy she had ever known, and that trait had paid off for him professionally and personally. A resolve that bordered on obstinacy had undoubtedly helped him cope with Ty's illness and keep the boy focused on recovery. No, if Jake Trahan was hell-bent on convincing her she had a place in his life, he would give it his all.

Well, it wouldn't work. She would see to that. The thing to do was to just stay away from him. Make sure he wasn't home when the boys studied together. Avoid the places he was likely to be. Just stay as far away from Jake as she possibly could.

And try not to think about him?

That was easier said than done, but she would do it. All she had to do was keep her mind occupied with something else. How hard could that be when she had a major renovation staring her in the face? Work, work, work. That was the solution. She would make sure there was no time or place in her life for Jake.

Feeling better with her new resolution in place, she pulled into the driveway at the back of Belle Terre, killed her engine and roused Cade. Groggily, he staggered to the back door and leaned against the wall, eyes closed, while he waited for her to find her keys.

"Be very quiet as you go upstairs," she told him, opening the door. "I don't want to wake your Uncle Drew."

His only response was a groan. She didn't even want to think about the response she would get when she woke him up in less than four hours to go to school. They made it through the house, up the stairs and into Cade's room without incident. Then Annabelle closed his door and started for her own room.

"Do you know what time it is?"

She turned to find Drew wearing only pajama pants,

standing in the darkened hall. "Late. I'll talk to you in the morning."

"It is morning."

"I told you that Cade and I might be out all night. You knew where we were."

Drew scrubbed his face with both hands. "With the sheriff."

"No. Chief of police. I was keeping an eye on his son while he was out on a call. Drew, I explained all of this on the phone."

He nodded. "Yeah, yeah. I remember now."

"Good. And good night."

"Hold on."

"No way. I'm too tired—" and too unnerved, she could have added "—to stand here and try to hold an intelligent conversation."

"I gotta tell you something. Dad—"

"Oh, Drew. You didn't tell him where I was, did you? I asked you—"

"Not to tell me that you were out gallivanting all over town until all hours of the night," said a voice from behind her. "I can see that for myself."

Annabelle turned to find her father looking unmussed from sleep and definitely not happy to see her.

"Your brother cares enough about you and your son, *and* your reputation, not to keep me in the dark," Philip informed her.

She shot Drew a look, then pasted on a tired smile for her father. "Hello, Daddy. I didn't know you were home."

"Obviously."

Well, that just about said it all. He didn't intend to let her get any rest until he had his say, so she might just as well get it over with.

"Drew," Philip said. "We can finish this alone."

As angry as Annabelle was at her brother for ratting on her, she winced at her father's curt dismissal. Poor Drew, she thought. He wasn't much better than she was at confronting the powerful Senator Delacroix. Without a word, Drew returned to his bedroom.

"Daddy," she said. "Can't we have this discussion in the morning?"

"I have a nine o'clock meeting in New Orleans tomorrow. Anyway—" he smoothed the lapel of his smoking jacket "—there'll be no 'discussion.' Jake Trahan and his son are off limits where you are concerned. In case you've forgotten—"

"I haven't forgotten a thing, and please keep your voice down. I don't want to wake Cade."

"I'm disappointed in you, Annabelle."

Oh, the dreaded disappointment. The fate worst than death that had kept her cowed most of her childhood and into adolescence. It was an old and reliable ploy, and one her father used with precision. "I'm sorry, but we both know this is not the first time. I doubt it will be the last."

"Not if you persist in this unseemly behavior."

"Unseemly? Dad, I know you're of the old school, but even you can't possibly find anything unseemly in baby-sitting a sick boy."

"The boy doesn't give me pause, but his father does."

"His father was gone."

"Don't insult my intelligence, Annabelle. You know very well that seeing Trahan under any circumstances is asking for trouble."

She didn't tell him that she had come to the same conclusion on her own. Pride prevented her from giving him the satisfaction of agreeing. "This is not worth arguing about."

"Of course not. It's only your reputation we're talking about." When she didn't respond, he said, "Then perhaps we can find something more worthwhile." The icy tone in his voice set off alarms in her head. "Like the fact that you have decided to totally disregard my wishes about going to work."

Drew again, she thought. My, but he'd been a real chatterbox. She felt a pang of sadness at the thought that she couldn't trust her brother to keep a promise.

"I told you that I intended to get a job."

"Job? This...notion of yours hardly qualifies as a job. Really, Annabelle. Managing a hotel? Oh, not that the Delacroix name wouldn't be a draw for something like that, but it's not exactly what I wanted for you."

"You mean it's not as grand as being hostess of Belle Terre?"

"Frankly, yes."

Her head was hurting and her eyes stung from lack of sleep. "Daddy, I had hoped to have this conversation under more pleasant circumstances, not to mention broad daylight, but since you've brought it up..." She took a deep breath. "If you want a hostess, hire one. If you don't approve of my career plans, I'm sorry, but I'm going ahead. If you're concerned that I'll somehow tarnish the Delacroix name, well...I'm not sure I even want to address that. Now, I'm extremely tired and I'm going to bed. If you want to discuss this further, I'll be happy—"

"That won't be necessary. I can see that you've decided to do exactly as you wish, regardless of my feelings on the subject."

"Good night, Daddy." She started toward her bedroom.

"In time you'll see that I'm right. In time you'll see that your place is here."

Annabelle didn't even dignify his attitude with a response. She was too damned tired.

As Philip Delacroix watched his youngest daughter disappear into her bedroom, he knew she was making a mistake. Just as he knew it was up to him to prevent it. Just as he knew that when all was said and done, she would do as she always had. Obey him.

CHAPTER SEVEN

"I DON'T UNDERSTAND," Annabelle said, feeling as if someone had just tossed a bucket of ice water in her face. "Just a few days ago you told me that there would be no problem with my loan. And now you're turning me down. What's changed since then?"

On the other side of the massive mahogany desk, Walton Ambrose, vice president of the Bayou Bank and Trust, cleared his throat. "Well, the, uh, loan committee feels that the stocks you've offered as collateral aren't stable enough to insure the amount of the loan."

"Aren't stable enough?" She couldn't believe it. "Those stocks have paid dividends consistently for the last seven years. What more could they ask for?"

"You have to understand, Mrs. Rowland. You're talking about a venture that might possibly pay off. On the other hand, you could go broke in six months."

His casual attitude infuriated her. Could it be that after all the forms she had filled out, all the questions she had answered, he'd concluded that her plan was just some whim of a bored divorcée? Be calm, she told herself. Be professional. If she wanted to be treated like a businesswoman, she had to act like one. She couldn't believe the man needed a lesson in state economics, but he was either misinformed or uninformed.

"Mr. Ambrose, tourism in Louisiana is big business," she said, stating what she considered to be the obvious. "Particularly in this area. Between New Orleans, the racetracks, casinos, antebellum homes and swamp tours, people flock here in droves. Since the hotel closed, there's no place between Slidell and Covington on Interstate 12 for tourists to stay. Mandeville has accommodations, but they're even farther off the interstate than we are. I've done my research, Mr. Ambrose. Bayou Beltane can easily support a bed-and-breakfast of the size I've proposed."

Suddenly he smiled. "Well now, the hotel is the perfect example of why this venture is just too risky," he told her.

Great, she thought. Here she was trying to convince him, and all she'd done was give him the perfect cannonball to fire holes in her plan.

"The closing of the hotel should tell you that your research is flawed. There simply wasn't enough business to keep it open. What makes you think you, with no experience, could do better?"

"Because, if you'll pardon my frankness, the hotel was a dump. And word of mouth is still one of the most effective forms of advertising. Positive and negative. I've talked to the mayor, the city inspector and the former manager of the hotel, and they all confirm the fact that the absentee owner's lack of attention was the major problem. He failed to make necessary repairs. The plumbing was terrible and the food service was worse. You can't possibly compare the two establishments. I will be living on the property, caring for my guests."

"I'm sorry, Mrs. Rowland. But the bank feels you don't have enough of a track record to risk fifty thousand dollars. Now, if you were to have someone cosign for you...say, your father...then—"

"No. My father won't be co-signing anything for me." Her father was the last person she wanted involved in her business. And even if she did, she doubted he would be willing, considering the cold shoulder he'd given her since the night of their confrontation. "Won't you please reconsider, Mr. Ambrose?"

"Not at this time, I'm afraid. Have you considered the Small Business Administration?"

"Yes." That was certainly a viable option. If she wanted to wait until Cade graduated from high school before opening her business.

"Of course, they move much slower than a bank. And I understand the paperwork is horrendous, but the interest rates are low."

"Yes." Annabelle rose to leave, but stopped after several steps toward the door. She turned back to Mr. Ambrose. If they wouldn't go the full amount, maybe they would approve a lesser sum. She'd hoped to use her stocks only as collateral, and the dividends would help out until the B and B started making money. Now maybe she'd have to sell her stocks, after all. "You said I didn't qualify for fifty thousand. Does that mean I qualify for less?"

"Well, I…"

"Will the bank loan me forty thousand, or even thirty?"

"Uh, no."

"Twenty-five? That's half the amount I originally asked for."

"I'm really sorry, Mrs. Rowland, but not even that much."

Not only no, but hell no, she thought, disappointed

and disgusted. But she managed a polite smile. "Thank you for your time, Mr. Ambrose."

He smiled back, then added insult to injury. "Have a nice day."

By the time Annabelle stepped out of the bank she was so mad she wanted to scream. Obviously Bayou Bank and Trust didn't want her business. Neither did the First Bank of Covington or the St. Tammany Savings and Loan, where she had also applied for a loan. Three strikes in as many days. But why? She was missing something obvious. Something she should do, or something she shouldn't have done. Whatever it was, she needed a fresh pair of eyes to look at the problem.

The first name that came to mind was Drew, but she quickly dismissed him. She'd forgiven him for telling her father everything, but she had to admit there was still tension between them. The next person she thought of was Joanna, but she wasn't sure of the welcome she would receive. Going to her sister would mean eating a little crow. Not that Joanna would demand it, but Annabelle knew that her sister had spoken some truths at their last meeting. She also knew she had jumped to their father's defense so quickly and adamantly, she had left Joanna little choice but to let the matter rest unless she was willing to start yet another family feud. Feuding wasn't Joanna's style. She was levelheaded and fair. Two of the qualities that made her an excellent candidate to help with the problem.

So, how important was the bed-and-breakfast? Annabelle asked herself. Important enough to go to Joanna with her hat in her hand, so to speak? She took a deep breath. *Just give me a hat.*

THE OFFICES OF Delacroix and Associates were quiet and orderly, the decor tasteful. Much like her Uncle

Charles, Annabelle thought, or at least her memories of him.

She smiled at the receptionist. "I'd like to see Joanna Gideon, please."

"Do you have an appointment?"

"No, but—"

"Annabelle."

She glanced up to see Shelby coming toward her. "Great to see you again. How are you doing?"

"Fine. I just stopped by to talk to Joanna for a moment."

"She's in a meeting." Shelby looked at her watch. "But she should be free in ten or fifteen minutes. Would you like to wait in my office?"

"I don't want to bother you. I can wait out here."

"Nonsense. You're family. C'mon." Shelby asked the receptionist to notify Joanna that her sister was in Shelby's office, then led the way.

"Very nice," Annabelle said when they were inside the small but comfortable room.

"Want a cup of coffee?"

"No, thanks. I don't want to keep you from your work. I remember enough about law firms to know the caseloads are sky-high."

"Always." Toying with a pencil, Shelby frowned. "I just wish my win-lose record was better."

"I wouldn't worry too much. You haven't been out of law school long enough to have much of a record either way."

"No, but you know me. I can't stand it when things don't pan out like they're supposed to, and I've got a case that's making me crazy. But then," she said absently, "the ones with kids always do."

"Not an abuse case, I hope."

Shelby shook her head. "Custody. But my client took off with the child, and now I can't even negotiate a reasonable settlement to help her retain custody."

"Poor thing, she must have been afraid she'd lose."

"Actually, what set her off was having to consider allowing visitation rights."

"That's not so unusual, is it? If the custody battle was nasty, she probably didn't want the ex-husband to have any influence in the child's life. People do some bizarre things when they've been hurt."

"She wasn't nearly as upset about the child's father having access to the child as she was the wife. In fact..." Shelby thought for a moment. "Now that you mention it, I recall her making several statements about the wife. Things like, 'I won't have my baby around that woman' and 'I'll do whatever it takes to keep him out of that woman's hands.'"

"Wicked Witch of the West, huh?"

"I don't think so, but then...I don't really know a lot about her." Shelby tapped the pencil against the desk. "Now, why would she be afraid of someone who appears so harmless?"

"The wicked witch?"

"No. My client."

Annabelle chuckled. "You lost me."

Shelby tossed the pencil aside and looked her cousin in the eye. "Why would my client be afraid for her child to be anywhere near the new wife?"

"Are you asking my opinion?"

"Help me out here," Shelby said, quite serious. "I'm just bouncing questions around and it helps to hear them out loud. You have a child. Put yourself in this situation. What would you be afraid of?"

"Probably that my child would be harmed in some way by this woman."

"What kind of harm?"

"Shelby, asking a parent about their fears for their child is like asking how high is up. Believe me, most parents are paranoid, anyway."

"I really want you to tell me," Shelby insisted.

Annabelle could see the concentration in her cousin's eyes. Clearly, Shelby had a direction in mind. "All right." She shrugged. "I'd want to be sure the woman had some character, some good qualities, not the least of which would be patience. Under that same heading, I'd want assurance that the woman wasn't involved with drugs or alcohol. Personally, I'd prefer she didn't even smoke. But it's hard to know what people do in private."

"I see what you mean. I also see that I've done my client an injustice, and there's no telling how long it would have gone on if we hadn't talked today. I want to thank you, Annabelle."

"Do you mind if I ask what for?"

Shelby smiled. "A new direction. I've been so focused on proving the father was a dirtball, I completely forgot about the wife. She looked okay on the surface and I never went any deeper. I let my client down."

"Shelby, don't be too hard on yourself. You—"

A knock at the door interrupted her.

"Come in," Shelby called, and in walked Joanna.

"Hi," she said warmly.

"Your sister is a genius," Shelby announced. "She may have just helped me solve my custody case."

"Really," Joanna said. "That's great."

Annabelle waved off the compliment. "I was in

town and thought I'd drop by." What a lie, she thought. And surely one her sister would see through.

"Glad you did."

"I'm not keeping you from a client, am I?"

"No. In fact, I've got time for a cup of coffee with my favorite sister."

Annabelle smiled, relieved. Why had she even hesitated to come to Joanna? Of all the people in her family, in her life at the moment, Joanna had always been the most understanding. And even though they hadn't had much of a relationship until they were grown, Joanna had become very special to her.

"Thanks for letting me hang out for a few minutes," Annabelle told Shelby.

"Are you kidding? I owe you big time. One of these days I'm taking you to a long, expensive lunch."

"I'm a witness," Joanna declared. "We'll hold her to it."

"See you later, Shelby," Annabelle said.

Joanna closed the door behind them and turned to Annabelle. "I'm so glad you stopped by, Annie."

"Me, too."

"I hated the way we left things between us," Joanna said as she ushered her sister into her office.

"I agree," Annabelle said with a deep sigh. They sat down on the lovely antique settee in one corner of Joanna's office. Annabelle stroked the brocade upholstery appreciatively. "This is a nice piece."

"Thanks. I knew you'd like it." Joanna's brows rose questioningly. "Something you want to talk about?"

Annabelle wasn't quite sure where to start. "This is going to sound like I'm running to my big sister at the first sign of a problem, but—"

"That's what big sisters are for. We didn't get a

chance to do a lot of that growing up, so I'm glad you feel comfortable coming to me. Is it about Drew?''

"No."

"Cade?"

"It's me. I've decided to start my own business."

Joanna's eyes twinkled with delight. "That's wonderful. What kind of business?''

"I want to buy the old Portier house and turn it into a bed-and-breakfast. I've had the house inspected. It's in pretty good shape. I've gotten estimates from several contractors and the work involved is fairly minimal. Cade and I will live there, of course, and—"

"Whoa," Joanna said. "Slow down."

"I...I just wanted you to know this wasn't some half-baked fantasy."

"Why would I think that? You're an intelligent woman. You have a flair for design. And as for the business part, well, you ran a household for years. You've told me yourself that you were the family accountant, you planned all of Neal's company functions. I'd say a bed-and-breakfast was right up your alley."

"You seem to be the only one. I need a loan to pull this off, and as of an hour ago, I've been turned down by the three largest lending institutions around. I thought maybe you might be able to give me some options I hadn't considered."

"How much do you need?"

"Fifty thousand."

"That's not exactly asking for the moon. Where did you go?''

When Annabelle stated the names of the banks and loan companies she'd approached, Joanna frowned. "Does Dad know about your plans?''

"Yes."

"And I take it he isn't pleased."

"No."

Joanna leaned back against the settee and looked straight into Annabelle's eyes. "I meant what I said, Annie. I'm truly glad that you came to me, and I don't want our relationship to be strained."

"Neither do I."

"What I'm about to suggest may be difficult for you to hear, but I want you to know there's no malice intended." She paused for a moment. "There's a possibility that Dad may be the reason you can't get a loan."

Shocked, Annabelle opened her mouth to speak, then closed it. The last time she and Joanna had a discussion about their father, she had jumped to his defense out of guilt. This time she took a minute to collect her thoughts before responding. "What do you mean?"

"He personally knows every banker within three hundred miles. He could have, well, let's just say he could have suggested that your idea was a flash in the pan. A bad risk."

"That's a horrible accusation."

"And I wish I didn't even have to consider it, but I do."

"Why would he deliberately try to sabotage my efforts?"

"To keep you under his thumb. To keep you at Belle Terre."

As soon as the words were spoken, Annabelle knew there was more than a grain of truth in what Joanna said. Still, it was difficult to believe her own father would do such a thing.

"Don't you think that's a bit drastic?"

"Yes."

The single word answer couldn't have been more

damning. Joanna considered Philip totally capable of sabotaging his own daughter's dreams.

"He wants you to play hostess, doesn't he?" Joanna asked.

"I told him it wasn't for me."

"And then your loan was rejected."

"One doesn't necessarily have anything to do with the other," Annabelle insisted, even while her suspicions mounted.

Joanna leaned forward and put her hand on her sister's. "Don't take too much at face value where Dad is concerned. He always has an agenda. Don't forget that. Now," she said, her tone brightening, "let's see what we can do about getting your venture financed. Do you have a prospectus of some kind?"

"What?"

"A prospectus. A game plan. Something an investor can look at."

"An investor?"

"As a matter of fact, if your proposal looks as good as I think it will, I might be interested in backing you myself."

"Oh, now wait a minute, Joanna. I didn't come in here looking for a handout." She wouldn't take charity.

"And I'm not offering one. But Richard did leave me quite a lot of money, and I see no reason for you to go to a bank when I can loan you whatever amount you need."

Annabelle was deeply touched. "I really appreciate the offer, but—"

"It would give me a lot of pleasure to do this for you."

"I can see that, and believe me, that's worth more than any amount of money. But I want to do this without any help from the family. I want to be able to look back and say I did it on my own. Can you understand?''

''Completely. And I'm so proud of you,'' Joanna said, pride shining in her eyes. ''Looks like my baby sister is all grown up.''

''The jury is still out on that one.''

''Well, I think I can help sway the verdict. I know several, shall we say, independent financiers in New Orleans who might be interested in your venture. Why don't you let me give them a call—''

''Could you give me their names instead?''

Joanna smiled. ''On your own, right?''

''Right.''

ANNABELLE SPENT the following day in New Orleans, talking to the bankers Joanna had recommended. She returned to Bayou Beltane with a handful of applications and a heart full of hope. In fact, she was so hopeful and pleased with herself that she didn't notice Cade was being unusually quiet when she picked him up from school.

''Mom,'' he said when they were halfway to Belle Terre. ''Could I ask you a question?''

The fact that he was asking permission told her the nature of the question was serious, at least to him. ''Always.''

''If I asked you to do something real important, and asked you not to tell Ty's Dad, would you?''

''I don't know, Cade. I really can't give you an answer until I know what it is.''

He thought about it for a moment or two, then said, ''Ty wants to go ahead and get his head shaved. He thinks his hair really looks gross. And he hates those baseball caps, so he figured he's gonna be bald, anyway, why not just got ahead and do it now.''

"I think that's perfectly understandable. And I doubt Jake would object if—''

"No, it's not that, it's just that…'' He frowned, as if trying to find the right words to explain.

"What?''

"This is the part you gotta promise not to tell.''

"All right.''

"He doesn't want his dad to come in with him. He thinks it'll be hard for him to, you know—'' Cade shrugged ''—stand there and watch them shave his head. Anyway, Ty says his dad's been through a lot, what with Ty's mom dying and then resigning as sheriff and moving and everything, so he figures he doesn't need the stress and …'' He took a deep breath. "Would you drive him?''

Annabelle almost said no. Every time she was with Ty, the more she liked him, the more she wanted to mother him. Not good. Then she thought about how important this obviously was to him. She had successfully avoided Jake for the better part of a week, four days to be exact, but who was counting. Surely she could help Ty without much danger of running into Jake.

"I'd be honored.''

Cade's face split in a wide grin. "Today?''

"We're almost home.''

"Yeah, but I sorta told him we could…maybe do it today.''

Annabelle pulled over to the shoulder, waited for a truck to pass, then executed a U-turn. "You owe me one, pal.''

He gave her the thumbs-up sign. "Cool.''

They drove back into town, picked up Ty and headed for the barber shop, which was a couple of doors away from the Book Nook. "Okay," she told the boys. "You guys go do your thing, then meet me in the bookstore." She ruffled Cade's thick locks. "Wouldn't hurt you to get a trim while you're at it."

He held out his hand. "I need money."

"Don't we all." She handed him a twenty-dollar bill. "And bring back the change, please," she called as they took off. Without looking back, Cade waved the money in response.

Annabelle browsed through the well-stocked shelves of the Book Nook and selected a couple of books on Victorian architecture and furniture of the period, and even one on making Victorian craft items using Battenburg lace. Pleased with her finds, she paid for the books and left. She had just deposited her purchases in her car and locked it when Jake whipped his cruiser into the parking space next to her.

He got out and walked toward her. "Hi."

How could a man get better looking in four days? It wasn't possible, was it? Of course, it could be that she had missed his smile, missed him. "Hello, Jake."

"I got Ty's note."

She really should stop staring at him, she told herself. But he was so wonderful to look at. So handsome. For the first time in her life she fully understood the saying "There's nothing like a man in uniform." Jake looked spectacular in his. The dark blue deepened the color of his eyes to forest green, cool and inviting.

"Where is he?"

"What?"

"I got Ty's note saying he was with you. Where is he?"

''Oh, well...we've done something without asking you first, and I hope you don't mind.''

''Won't know until you tell me.''

''Ty wanted to go ahead and have his head shaved, and he asked if I would take him. Are you upset?''

Briefly, Jake glanced away. ''No. He mentioned doing it a couple of weeks ago and I probably should have taken him then, but I was a little worried about how his classmates would react. Kids can be pretty cruel sometimes. Aw, hell,'' he said. ''Truth is, I hated the idea of watching, so I put it off.''

''That's what Ty thought,'' Annabelle said softly.

''Kid's got a lot of guts, and he knows me too well.''

''He's very perceptive.''

''Yeah. Sometimes it's damned scary. His mother was like that. She *felt* things. Empathized with people. It was one of the traits that attracted me to her after...after you. That and her courage. Ty has that, too.''

''Jake—''

''It's the truth, Anna. There's no point in pretending otherwise. Alicia was a wonderful woman, and I loved her. But not the way I love you.''

The fact that he used the present tense didn't go unnoticed. How was she going to withstand the tide of emotion that swept through her whenever she saw him? Like now. Just a casual encounter on the street and she was torn between wanting to hear his words of love and knowing she had no right. She turned and took a couple of steps back to her car, but he cut her off.

''You can't run away forever, Anna.''

''Jake, please—''

''Please what? Stop loving you? If I haven't been able to do that in sixteen years, what makes you think I can stop now?''

She glanced around, almost hoping someone was watching. Anything for an excuse not to continue this conversation. "I can't—"

He touched her arm. "Yes, you can."

Behind them a bell tinkled as a shop door opened and closed. "Hey, Dad," she heard Ty say.

Jake looked up, and for a moment she couldn't decide if the expression on his face was one of shock or bewilderment. Then she thought she saw his eyes mist. She made a move to turn around, but he stopped her with a gentle pressure on her arm.

"Don't panic," he said, then slowly turned her around himself.

Annabelle gasped as Ty and Cade ambled toward them, smiles on their faces.

Both with their heads shaved. Totally bald. Slick and shiny as billiard balls.

"Oh, Cade," she whispered.

"Told you she was gonna freak out," he told Ty.

"It'll grow back," Ty said nervously.

"But why?"

Cade shrugged. "Just figured I'd look like Ty for a while. No big deal. Hey, can we go in the bookstore and see if they've got any comic books?"

Annabelle was too numb to answer.

"Sure, go ahead," Jake told them.

"Why?" she asked again. "He must know they'll both be the talk of the school tomorrow."

"He knows." Jake glanced down at her. "I thought *my* son was just about the gutsiest kid I'd ever known. Until today."

CHAPTER EIGHT

My son. My son.

Every time Annabelle looked at Cade, Jake's words haunted her. Both his sons were courageous. Tears still filled her eyes when she thought of the sacrifice Cade had made for his half brother. It was even more meaningful since Ty was only able to attend school three, sometimes four days a week. The rest of the time Cade was on his own with his gloriously bald head.

After she and Jake had gotten over the initial shock, the four of them had gone out for pizza. Ty and Cade had strolled into Rick's sporting their bald heads like badges of honor, which indeed they were, ignoring any and all curious glances and raised eyebrows. When they left the restaurant later, Jake thanked Cade and shook his hand. Not a grown-up-to-a-teenager handshake, but man to man. Cade dismissed the whole affair as if it were nothing so great, but she saw his eyes shine, and the way he looked up at Jake. Almost worshipful.

The way a son would look at his father.

Stop it! Torturing herself this way wasn't doing anyone any good. She had to prevent her mind from dwelling on such things. But late at night, like now, those thoughts crowded in, clung like seaweed to driftwood. As she stood on the veranda looking out at the moon glistening on the bayou, stars shining in a velvet sky, she tried not to think of the years ahead as the bond of friendship between Ty and Cade grew stronger, which she knew would happen. Double dates. The prom. Graduation and maybe on to the same college. And all the time she would have to stand by, watching Jake, continuing the lie.

Annabelle ran her fingers through her hair, lifting it away from her neck. She wished she could lift the burden of her lie away as easily. Was she strong enough to keep up the pretense? Or maybe she should be asking herself if she was strong enough to give it up. Wouldn't it be great, she thought, if she could just wish on a star and everything would be wonderful.

"Star light, star bright," she whispered, letting her hair sift through her fingers, down over her shoulders, "first star I see tonight. I wish I may—"

"Let me know if that works, will you?"

She spun around to find her brother leaning against the door, his tie loosened, his suit coat thrown over one arm. "Drew, I didn't hear you come in."

"No. You were miles away." He pushed himself from the door and came toward her. "Anywhere but here, huh?"

"Why do you say that?"

He flung his coat over the back of one of the wrought-iron bistro chairs. "Still planning on moving out, aren't you."

"Not anytime soon. It seems I'm a bad risk."

"What does that mean?"

"My bank loan was turned down," she said flatly. "And before you recommend another bank, I've been to several. Same song, different verses."

"I'm sorry, sis."

Shadows made it impossible for her to see the expression on his face, but she heard the sincerity in his voice, and it was a comfort. "Thanks."

"You want it bad?"

"Yes, I do. I know you and Daddy don't agree with my ideas, but frankly, it doesn't matter. This is my dream, and yes, I want it bad."

"Well, I hope your wish comes true."

Maybe it was admitting out loud how much she wanted the bed-and-breakfast. Or maybe it was knowing that telling Drew was almost like telling her father. Whatever the reason, renewed strength and optimism surged through her.

"You know something?"

"What?"

"I've been wishing for things all my life, and damned few of them have come true. This time I'm not leaving it up to wishing and hoping. Somewhere, somehow, I'll get the money to buy my house, and I'll do it with plain old hard work. Not a wish in sight."

"Courage in the face of adversity. Not exactly one of our most prominent family traits, at least not this side of the family. But on you it looks good."

"Feels good." She touched his arm lightly. "You should try it sometime." Then she turned to go inside.

"Sis?"

She stopped at the door. "Yes?"

"You'll make it," he told her.

Annabelle smiled into the dark. "Yes. I will."

THE NEXT DAY she went to see Bud Snider, signed a contract and put down a deposit, "earnest money," on the Portier House. Her hand shook when she wrote the check that would ensure no one came along and bought the house out from under her, but when she had done it, she was relieved. And excited. She had taken the next step toward fulfilling her dream, and though she still felt a hefty dose of apprehension, she refused to allow it to overshadow her happiness. Key in hand, she left Bud Snider's office and drove over to Delacroix and Associates to share her excitement with Joanna. But to her supreme disappointment, her sister was in the New Orleans office and wouldn't be back until late afternoon.

Okay, Annabelle decided, she would just celebrate on her own. Leaving her car parked at the law firm, she walked into the heart of town. She could treat herself to lunch, but eating alone didn't sound like much fun. Maybe she would call Jake and...

No. Bad idea, she told herself, but wasn't totally convincing. Just when she was about to decide there would be no one to share her news with until Cade got out of school, she glanced over to see Katherine Beaufort pull up in front of the antique store where they'd first met.

Perfect, Annabelle thought. The perfect person. She hurried across the street just as Katherine was getting out of her car.

"Hi there," she said.

"Well, hello." Katherine smiled. "Good to see you again."

"Running into you today must be providence or fate or something," Annabelle told her.

"How so?"

"I just put down earnest money on a new house. And not just any house. The Portier House Bed and Breakfast," she announced proudly. "And it's only fair that you should be the first to know, since you gave me the idea."

Katherine's eyes widened. "You're kidding?"

"Nope. There are still some wrinkles to be ironed out, and a lot of hard work ahead, but it's going to happen."

"Congratulations. I'll be your first customer."

Annabelle grinned. "I was counting on that."

"I'm so excited for you. What am I saying? I'm excited for me, too," Katherine said, laughing. "This calls for a celebration."

"I agree."

"I have an appointment to look at some estate items in Covington around two, but in the meantime, I'd love to buy lunch for Bayou Beltane's newest business-woman."

"I'd be delighted. Rick's is just around the corner. Have you ever been there?"

Katherine nodded. "Rick's it is. So, tell me about the house," she said as they started toward the restaurant.

Annabelle stopped. "Would you like to see it? My car isn't far from here."

"Oh, Annabelle. I'd love to."

Ten minutes later, Annabelle unlocked the door to the Portier House and ushered in her new friend.

"Lovely," Katherine said. "Absolutely lovely. This is quite a find."

"I know. It's been vacant for several years, but it's in good shape."

"This place will be stunning when you've got it furnished."

"Which will include several pieces from your shop, I hope. As a matter of fact," she said, an idea forming in her head, "I'm thinking about setting aside a corner of the library as a gift shop. You know, Victorian postcards, hand-painted boxes, dolls, that kind of thing. Would you and your partner be interested in putting some of your small pieces and decorator items in here?"

Katherine smiled warmly. "That idea has possibilities. I like the way you think. I'll have to confer with my partner, of course, but I think K & D's Antiques would be thrilled to have a spot in Portier House."

"Wonderful. Ready for the tour?"

As they wandered through the rooms, Annabelle shared her plans with Katherine, excited to exchange ideas with someone who visualized things the same way she did. The next hour flew by while they talked of iron beds, window treatments and Victorian bric-a-brac. They both agreed they could have spent the rest of the day talking, but Katherine had her appointment in Covington, so all too soon to suit Annabelle, they were back in town saying goodbye. As she was standing beside Katherine's car, Annabelle glanced across the street and saw Drew coming out of the Bayou Bank and Trust. Curious, she thought. Her father's firm did most of its business with Gulf States Bank.

"Thanks so much for showing me the house. I know you're going to be a success."

"What? Oh, yes," Annabelle said. For a moment she had forgotten Katherine was even there. "Thanks for coming with me."

Katherine glanced at her watch. "I've got to run. I'm sorry about lunch. How about a rain check?"

"That would be lovely."

"Let's make it next week, when you come to our shop."

"Perfect. I can't wait to see the sofa and armoire

you described. They sound exactly like the kind of pieces I'll need.''

"I'm looking forward to it. See you then.''

When Katherine waved goodbye and pulled out of the parking space, Annabelle glanced across the street again, but Drew was gone. Oh, well, she sighed, she was too pleased with her day to worry about her brother. She still had the key to the house, and before returning it to Bud Snider, she decided to go back and take some measurements. She reminded herself she could be jumping the gun since her financing wasn't actually in place. But at least two of the bankers she had talked to in New Orleans were enthusiastic about the project and supportive enough for her to feel certain the loan would go through. Feeling good, she climbed into her car and backed out of her parking place.

From the window of the florist shop, Jake watched Annabelle drive past and smiled. Bud Snider's secretary had called Miz Luella with the news of the earnest money, and by now it was probably all over town. Jake had to admit he'd been a little worried about her dream of making the B and B a reality. He'd been keeping tabs on her through Ty's friendship with Cade and knew she was having trouble securing enough money. He'd even considered offering her his help, then changed his mind, knowing she wouldn't accept. So, by God, she'd done it on her own, just as she said she would. He was so proud of her he could bust.

"Sheriff?"

He turned to the clerk. "Chief," he said automatically.

"Is this what you had in mind?" The woman set an arrangement of day lilies, carnations, baby's breath and greenery on the counter.

Jake eyed the flowers. Nice, but too generic, and definitely not romantic enough. "Changed my mind," he told the clerk. "I want one perfect—and it has to be perfect—long-stemmed red rose."

The lady gave him a look that said, *Bor-ing,* but he ignored it. So what if a single rose was a little corny? It meant true love, and that's exactly the message he wanted to convey. He had given Anna some space. Now it was time to make his move.

"WHAT AM I GOING TO DO with you?"

Annabelle almost jumped out of her skin at the unexpected sound of a man's voice behind her. The notebook and pencil in her hand went flying, landing on the hardwood floor. "Jake!" she cried, her hand at her throat. "You scared the living daylights out of me."

"I damn well better have scared the living daylights out of you. Anna, Bayou Beltane is a small town, and, thank God, small on crime, but if I catch you leaving this front door unlocked one more time, I swear I'm going to lock *you* up for your own protection."

"I'm sorry. You're right. I should've locked the door behind me, but I was so preoccupied with taking measurements and thinking about the placement of furniture that I..." She picked up the notebook and pencil and placed them on the mantel. "Well, I'm sorry. And I promise it won't happen again."

"Better not."

Her heart was still racing and she took a deep breath. "What are you doing here?"

He thought about giving her the rose, wrapped in crisp green florist's paper and lying on the front seat of his cruiser, but somehow this didn't seem like an appropriate time. "I knew you'd be here, and when I saw the door partially open—"

"How did you know I would be here?"

"Because you put earnest money down on this house today."

"And just how did you know that?"

"Telephone, telegram and tell Miz Luella. Fastest news service this side of the Mississippi."

"Some things never change."

"Well, look at it this way, saves subscribing to the newspaper."

Annabelle sighed. "I guess that also means everybody in town knows I was turned down by the banks when I tried to get a loan."

"Yeah. But you showed 'em. You hung in there. By the way, congratulations on the house."

"It's not mine yet."

"My money's on—" Jake's pager went off and he checked the digital readout.

"Trouble?" Annabelle asked.

"It's not an emergency, but I need to take care of it."

"You're never really off duty, are you."

Jake shook his head. "Fortunately, as I said, small town, small crimes. Gotta go." He started to walk away, then stopped. "Damn. I was hoping I'd be able to pick Ty up from school today."

"I'll do it when I pick Cade up," she offered.

"You sure? Because I can call Mrs. Segal."

The same Mrs. Segal he'd been talking to the night of the manhunt? Despite the fact that she knew she had no right to ask, her curiosity got the best of her. She just wasn't sure how to ask without sounding, well…jealous. "Listen, if she's already planned to pick him up, I wouldn't want to upset your friend's schedule.''

Jake thought he detected a hint of jealousy in her voice when she said "friend's," and he couldn't have been more pleased. "No problem." He waited a few seconds before adding, "At her age, I'm sure she'd rather spend time in her garden than in hauling a teenager, anyway.''

"Her age?''

"Didn't I tell you that she was a sixty-year-old grandmother?'' He tried to hide a grin. "Thought I had. Terrific lady, and a real sweetheart to agree to be my backup transportation and baby-sitter.''

"Oh. That's, uh, nice.''

"Hmm'' was his only comment. "I really appreciate you doing this, Annabelle. Seems I'm racking up quite a debt to you.''

"Don't be silly. I don't mind in the least. Ty's a delight.''

Jake looked at her and allowed his grin full range. "Yeah. He likes you, too.'' He leaned over and gave her a quick kiss on the lips. "He's got good taste, like his old man.'' Then, before she could protest the compliment or the kiss, he left, still grinning. Annabelle watched him go, wishing with all her heart that she could accept his kisses as freely as he gave them. How easy it would be to let Jake love her. How easy and wonderful. But she cared too deeply to let that happen. She knew he would continue to take little opportunities to remind her of what they'd once had. Persistence had won her the first time; she was certain he was counting on it again. But she had to be strong. She couldn't let her own needs dictate her behavior. She had to think about Jake and Ty, as well as Cade. Each day that passed, each moment Cade spent with Ty was a risk. The tangled web she had woven for herself had ensnared all of them. Her fleeting moment of jealousy at the thought that Jake might be more than friends with another woman was a warning. She was getting too close to the flame again. Too close to wanting what she couldn't have.

Just stay away from the fire, she told herself, locking the front door, then walking toward her car. She would insist on a friendship only, and sooner or later Jake would back down. Or would he? she asked herself, his words echoing in her head.

I'm not going to give up on us.

As she picked up the boys and drove to Jake's house, she thought about how determined he could be. But this was one time she couldn't allow him to win.

You said there is no us. But you're wrong. There is. There always has been. And I intend to do my best to make you believe that.

She didn't doubt him for a minute, she thought, pulling into his driveway. If it wasn't for Cade's relationship with Ty...

Oh, who was she kidding? That was a cop-out and she knew it. Even now, walking into his house, she knew she should take Cade and go home. Ty was having a good day so there was no need for her to stay. Just go, she told herself. But instead, she lingered until Ty and Cade started their homework. No sense interrupting them right in the middle of their assignments. Break their concentration. What was another half hour? She could still be gone by the time Jake got home. Couldn't she? Maybe?

By the time an hour had passed, the boys were still deep into biology and she decided she should call Belle

Terre. She didn't feel she had to keep Drew informed of her whereabouts, but a lifetime of good manners dictated that she at least let the staff know if, or when, she and Cade would be home for dinner. Mae answered the phone.

"Oh, no, ma'am," the maid replied when Annabelle asked if Drew was expected for dinner. "He's gonna be in N'awlins for the evenin'."

"Well then, I think Cade and I will eat dinner in town. Were there any calls for me?"

"Yes m'am. A Mr. Ambrose called. Said it was right important you call him as soon as possible."

"Thank you, Mae," Annabelle said, and hung up. What could Walton Ambrose want with her? Surely his call had nothing to do with the loan. He'd made the bank's position clear enough, she thought, lifting the phone to slide the telephone book from beneath it. She flipped through the yellow pages, found banks, then dialed the number for the Bayou Bank and Trust.

"I'm so glad you called, Mrs. Rowland," Ambrose said as soon as she was put through. "I've been giving serious consideration to our conversation the other day and, well...I have some good news. The bank has decided to approve your loan."

"My...you're going to...why?" she blurted. "I mean...not that I'm not grateful. I am. More grateful than I can say, but—"

Ambrose cleared his throat. "I have a little confession to make, Mrs. Rowland. Some of my fellow officers felt I had acted hastily when I turned down your application. They reminded me that you weren't just anybody off the street, but a Delacroix. Your family has been a part of Bayou Beltane's business community for over a hundred years, and if I forgot that, I apologize. Our bank would be pleased to have your business. Could you come in around ten tomorrow morning to finalize the necessary paperwork?''

Flabbergasted, Annabelle could hardly believe his change of heart, but she certainly wasn't going to question it. "Ten o'clock would be fine. And thank you, Mr. Ambrose.''

"No, thank you for your gracious acceptance.''

She hung up the phone and was staring at it when Cade walked into the kitchen. "Ty wants some juice. Mom," he said when she didn't respond. "Hey, Mom."

"We got it.''

"Yeah, sure. It's probably in the fridge.''

"We got it!'' she cried, her eyes wide and teary. "Cade, we got it!''

"Jeez, Mom, it's just—''

She grabbed him and hugged him. "We got the loan.''

"The loan for the house? No kiddin'?'' He hugged her back, and they held on to each other, jumping up and down, chanting, "We got it! We got it!''

"Got what?'' Ty asked, walking in on the scene.

"That's what I want to know," Jake asked as he came through the door.

"The loan!'' Cade and Annabelle said in unison. Then everybody started talking and laughing at once.

"THIS WAS A GREAT IDEA,'' Annabelle said. It had been Jake's idea to have a celebration dinner with take-out food and drinks from Rick's, served by candlelight on a rickety card table with folding chairs.

In the middle of the Portier House dining room.

The illumination from the dozen or so candles

perched on windowsills cast long shadows on the walls, making the room look like a set from an old horror movie. Once they had finished eating, the boys had set off to explore the second floor, flashlights in hand. As Jake and Annabelle cleaned up, they could hear their heavy footsteps overhead with an occasional ghostly moan or two thrown in for good measure.

"They're sure enjoying themselves," Jake commented.

"A couple of teenage boys and a creaky old house. Guess it doesn't get any better, huh?"

"Not unless you throw in a couple of teenage girls."

"I don't know about you, but I'm in no hurry to start down that road," she said, stuffing the food containers into a garbage bag.

He walked up behind her and leaned close. "At least not while I still hope to travel it myself."

She smelled the rose before she saw it, the fragrance swirling around her as he brought the flower from behind his back to present it to her. "I've been trying to find a moment to give this to you all day and finally decided the only right time was now."

"Jake," she whispered, taking the rose and turning around to face him. "Where in the world—"

"I brought it in when I hauled in the table and chairs. Hid it in the shadows."

She held the flower to her nose, slowly inhaling. "Thank you. It's lovely."

"So are you."

There was an odd yet disturbingly familiar fluttering in her stomach. "It's just the candlelight."

"No," he said, sliding his hand to the back of her neck, urging her closer. "It's you." He leaned down and caught her lower lip between his teeth. When he felt her shudder, he turned the nip into a slow, deep kiss.

Clutching the rose, she put her hand on his chest, supposedly to push him away, but it didn't happen. Instead with her other hand she grabbed at his shirt and held on. With a sound that was somewhere between a moan and a sigh, she leaned into him, into the kiss. She felt her body throbbing at every pulse point, felt her instincts shoving reason aside. Need bloomed inside her. So much need it threatened to overwhelm her, sweep her away in its powerful current.

"I need you," Jake whispered, kissing her mouth, her cheek.

Hearing him speak the words helped drag her back to reality. "The boys—"

"Are upstairs, and we'll hear them long before they see us." He kissed her again, pressing her body to his so that he felt every line and curve.

"We...shouldn't..." But her arms were around his neck, the fingers of her free hand tangled in his hair.

"Yes." He pressed his mouth to her throat. "We should. We will."

"Jake, Jake..." She was going to tell him something, insist on something, but for the life of her, she couldn't remember what it was. Her heart was beating so fast and so loud, she wondered why it didn't echo in the empty hallway.

Slowly, Jake ended the kiss, and her arms fell from his neck to hang limply at her sides.

He reached out and caressed her cheek. "Anna—"

There was a thundering of footsteps on the stairs and they moved apart.

"This is one cool place, Miz Rowland," Ty announced as he and Cade rejoined them.

"Thank you." She turned away, glancing around as if surveying the area for any remains of their picnic. "Well," she announced, putting her hands on her hips to hide the fact that they were shaking, "I don't think we left much behind for the mice."

"Hey, Cade, how about helping me carry the table and chairs back out to my car?" Jake asked. "Ty, maybe you could take that trash out. There's probably a barrel in the alley." The boys took up their tasks, and when they were gone, Jake turned to Annabelle. She started to say something, but he cut her off.

"Don't even think about telling me that what just happened was a mistake. We've covered that before. And if you're planning on using the boys as an excuse, you can forget that, too. They're not always going to be around. Sooner or later, it's just going to be you and me, Anna. You and me." He picked up the table and remaining chairs and headed outside.

That's exactly what she was afraid of. The last few minutes were proof positive that she had overestimated her willpower. She couldn't be alone with Jake. It was simply too dangerous. Delicious, she sighed, but dangerous.

As she stood in the softly lit room, the minutes seemed to drag by, and she wondered what was keeping Jake and Cade. A tiny flash of anxiety skittered along her nerve endings, but she refused to allow it to mushroom into panic. There was no reason to think there was anything out of the ordinary. But when a few minutes passed and Ty returned, but still no Jake and Cade, her nervousness threatened to overwhelm her. What could they be saying to each other? Then she heard steps on the hardwood floor of the entryway and sighed with relief. But Cade had an odd expression on his face and was strangely quiet.

"Well, thanks for the dinner," she said. "I hate to run, but it is a school night." Truthfully, she wanted to know if something had happened while Jake and Cade were outside.

"Anytime. And congratulations."

"Thanks."

"Yeah," Ty added. "Neat house. See ya, Cade."

"Yeah. See ya." Those were the first words Cade had spoken since walking back into the house with Jake. Annabelle was relieved when they were in the car and on their way back to Belle Terre.

"You tired?" she asked him.

"Nope."

Several minutes slipped by until she could no longer stand the suspense. "You and Jake were gone quite a while putting the table and chairs in the car."

"Yeah. We were talking."

"Oh?"

"Mom, do you still love Dad?" he asked out of the blue.

For a moment she toyed with the idea of lying to him, then decided against it. She had too many lies to deal with already; she didn't want to add one more to the list.

"No," she said softly, quickly glancing in his direction. As the lights from the oncoming traffic flickered across his face, she saw both sadness and understanding in his eyes. "Does that upset you?"

"Kinda. But in a way it doesn't, 'cause I don't think Dad loves us anymore."

Annabelle swallowed the knot in her throat and her eyes stung with tears. "Why do you say that?"

"He never calls. And when I call him, he's always gotta go or got a call on the other line."

"I'm sorry, Cade. I know that hurts."

"Not as much as it used to."

She figured that was only partially true, and said mostly for her benefit. "Do you mind if I ask what brought all this up?"

"I just wanted to know, 'cause if you still loved him, then you wouldn't wanna spend time with somebody else. You know, like on a date."

"A date?"

"Yeah. You're not too old to date, and you're still pretty."

"Thanks. I think."

"Well, that's what Jake and I were talking about. He said he wanted to ask me first, kinda like getting my permission."

"Permission?"

"Yeah. He wanted to know how I would feel if you and he went out on a date."

The car almost swerved into the other lane before Annabelle brought it under control. "If...if he and..."

"You know, like to a movie or something."

"And...and what did you tell him?"

Cade looked at his mother. "I said it's okay with me, if it's okay with you."

CHAPTER NINE

SHE'D UNDERESTIMATED JAKE. Not only was he determined to show her they belonged together, he had enlisted Cade's help to do it. And probably Ty's, as well. Three against one. She would have to keep her guard up.

Oh, sure. Like she had last night?

A few candles, a rose, and she had tumbled into his arms so fast she was still dizzy from the fall. And his lips. His caress...

Annabelle forced herself to concentrate on making a list of things to do. In an hour she had an appointment at the bank to sign the loan papers, then an appointment with Bud Snider to set up a closing for the house, and finally a meeting with the carpenter she had hired to go over the work she needed done. She had plenty to keep her busy. And out of Jake's path.

The phone rang once, twice. She picked it up on the third ring, wondering why one of the maids hadn't answered it. "Hello."

"Good morning."

"Jake."

"I was hoping for a little more enthusiasm, considering I'm the man taking you to dinner tonight."

"Dinner? No, I—"

"Don't even think the word, *can't*. I've made arrangements to have the evening off, and you and I are going out to dinner. We're driving into Covington and I promise you a nice, relaxed meal, nothing fancy. Then I'm going to drive you home and kiss you good-night.''

"Jake, I don't think—"

"You might as well say yes, because if you don't, I'm coming to Belle Terre and parking myself at your table. And I'm still going to kiss you good-night. So you see, one way or the other, you and I are having dinner together. Your choice.''

"I don't remember you being such a bully," she said, trying to sound offended and missing the mark.

"I prefer to think of it as being determined, but when it comes to you, the name doesn't matter. What does matter is that I'm not going to take no for an answer."

She kept remembering the look in his eyes last night when he'd told her, *Sooner or later it's just going to be you and me, Anna. You and me.* They hadn't even been completely alone last night and he had been hard enough to resist. How in the world would she be able to manage when it was only the two of them?

"This is just dinner, Anna. In a public restaurant," he said, as if reading her mind. He waited.

She was a grown woman with a mind and will of her own. All she had to do in order to remember there was no future for them was to think about Cade. "Just friends having dinner."

"I'll pick you up at six-thirty."

At the thought of him coming to Belle Terre, she panicked. "I can meet you—"

"No." Flat. Firm. "I'll pick you up at six-thirty." The fact that he knew Philip Delacroix was out of town would make it easier on Anna, Jake thought, though he didn't give a damn if the old man was there or not. He still would have called for her.

When he hung up, Jake reached for his coffee cup—and noticed how badly his hands were shaking. He wasn't sure what he would have done if she'd turned him down. Thank God she hadn't.

He used both hands to lift the cup to his lips. Maybe he should have let her off the hook about coming to Belle Terre. No, he decided. They'd had enough of that sixteen years ago. He was going to date Anna openly, no matter what her father or anybody else thought. He only wished to hell he'd had this much backbone all those years ago. If he had, maybe things would have turned out much differently. Then he thought about Ty. Jake would never have wanted to miss out on having one of the most wonderful sons a man could ask for. And he was sure Annabelle felt the same about Cade.

Ty and Cade. Jake thought about the way the two boys had become friends so fast. He'd never seen Ty befriend anyone the way he had Cade. And the same seemed to be true for Cade. They complemented each other. Where Ty had a tendency to be reflective, Cade was more physical. The relationship had been good for both of them, and he had to admit he was drawn to Cade in a way he'd never experienced with any of Ty's other friends.

Jake remembered the startled expression on Cade's face when he'd asked permission to take Anna out. And the pride when he'd explained that he was asking Cade because he was the man in the family and it was only right. The kid had struggled with his emotions for a moment, then he had looked Jake straight in the eye and said yes. They shook hands, and he could tell the boy was pleased.

Jake was thrilled. Asking permission had been a spur-of-the moment idea, and frankly, he hadn't stopped to consider what he would have done if Cade had said no, any more than he had when he broached the subject with Ty. Both boys seemed to accept his dating Anna, and neither saw it as a threat to their feelings for their missing parent. They had displayed an astonishing level of maturity. Jake smiled, making a mental note to do his best to stop thinking of them as boys.

HE WAS FEELING MORE like a teenager every second, Jake thought as he pulled into the circular drive in front of Belle Terre. Only once since moving back to St. Tammany Parish had he been inside the grand old plantation house. As sheriff-elect, he had been invited to a political function here that rivaled a Mardi Gras ball. Jake had never seen so much food and liquor, and so many attractive, affectionate women in one place in his life. He didn't like Philip Delacroix enough to spit on him if he was on fire, but the old bird threw one helluva party. Jake had stayed just long enough to put in an appearance, then gone home. He doubted anybody had missed him, least of all Delacroix.

Having abandoned the cruiser for the evening, Jake parked his own car and made his way up the front steps to ring the bell. The butler, Clovis, opened the door. "Good evening, sir."

"Good evening. Will you tell Mrs. Rowland...?"

"You're expected, sir."

Jake turned to the butler and was momentarily taken aback when he noticed the old man's left eye was brown while the other was pale and filmy, as if it had been damaged somehow. The contrast was startling, almost eerie. The unusual eyes, combined with a café-au-lait-colored skin and a shock of snow white hair were disconcerting to say the least.

"Would you care to wait in the parlor?" Clovis asked.

Jake shrugged. "This is fine."

Clovis nodded and left him alone in the parlor.

Impressive was the word that instantly came to mind as he stepped into the foyer of Belle Terre. Even though he had been here before, he realized that the huge crowd the night of the political function had obscured the size and the grandeur of the stately home. The sweeping staircase alone was enough to make visitors stop and stare. Looking like something out of a Civil War epic, it curved gracefully to the second story. The hand-carved newel post, caps and cove moldings were works of art in themselves.

Yeah, Jake thought, pretty grand, all right. But definitely not his taste. He thought about Riverwood, Charles Delacroix's house. The two residences reflected both the brothers' life-styles and the way they wanted the world to perceive them. He had been to Riverwood many times, and even though it was much smaller, less grand, it felt like a home. For all its stately distinction, Belle Terre felt more like a museum than a home. Funny, but all those years ago when he and Anna had been sneaking around, meeting in secrecy, he had longed to be welcomed inside. Now he couldn't wait to leave. And he definitely couldn't imagine Anna living the rest of her life here.

"Jake."

He turned around and found her standing in the entrance to the parlor. "Wow," he said. "You look gorgeous."

"Thank you." She would never admit she had changed no less than four times before deciding on the moss green column dress that flattered her figure, if she did think so herself. "You said nothing fancy. I hope I'm not overdressed."

Only in so much as it would give his imagination a delightful challenge to visualize what she would look like undressed. Cool it, he reminded himself. "You're perfect," he assured her.

She could have said the same for him. Although she loved the way he looked in his uniform, she had to admit that he was every bit as appealing in the tan slacks and navy shirt he wore tonight. He was quite simply the best-looking man she had ever seen. Behind her, someone cleared his throat. She turned and found Cade holding a plate of pizza in his hand.

"Hey, Cade," Jake greeted him.

"Hi." He looked at his mother. "You look nice."

"Thanks."

"More of a compliment than I got from Ty," Jake commented. "He told me I looked dull."

Cade laughed. "He was probably ticked that he had to stay with a baby-sitter."

"Mrs. Segal's not really a baby-sitter. It's just that until Ty gets well, I'm not comfortable leaving him alone at night. Besides, he still needs to get plenty of rest."

"He coulda come over here."

"Oh, sure," Annabelle interjected. "I can just imagine how much rest he would have gotten."

"By the way—" Jake handed Cade a piece of paper "—I'm taking your mom to the Ranch Steak House in Covington. That's the phone number in case you need us."

When Cade's face split in a wide grin, Annabelle asked, "What's so funny?"

"Well, you always wanna make sure where I am, and now I get to keep tabs on you. Now, don't forget to be careful, and remember what time you gotta be home," he instructed, enjoying himself immensely.

Jake put his hand at the small of Annabelle's back and urged her toward the door. "Let's get out of here before he docks your allowance."

THE RESTAURANT JAKE had selected was a small upscale steakhouse that offered patrons the option of selecting the actual cut of beef to be prepared for their dinner. The steaks were cooked on a huge indoor circular grill built in the center of the dining room. The atmosphere was exactly what Jake had promised. Quiet, relaxed. While they ate, he filled her in on several of the people in their graduating class who were still in the parish, the new civic projects on the horizon and his own plans for upgrading the police department. She told him the status of the house and about her trip into New Orleans the next day to look at some possible antiques for the B and B. Good, pleasant dinner conversation, making for a thoroughly enjoyable evening.

But as the evening wore on, Annabelle began to remember the terms of Jake's invitation. He'd promised quiet and relaxation, and he'd certainly delivered in style.

He'd also promised to kiss her good-night.

All through coffee and dessert, she kept thinking about how the evening would end. So much so, that when he called for the check her nerves jangled. They left the restaurant, drove back to Bayou Beltane and on to Belle Terre, and with every mile anticipation stretched her nerves tighter. When would he kiss her? As soon as he stopped the car or when he walked her to the door?

"Would you like to walk around back and sit on the veranda for a while?" she asked as soon as they started for the front door.

"Sounds nice."

They headed to the back of the house and Jake pulled out one of the wrought-iron bistro chairs for her.

"Can I get you something to drink?" she asked.

"No, thanks." He didn't sit, but shoved his hands into his pockets and gazed around the veranda and well-tended garden that gradually gave way to the natural foliage. "You know, when I was a kid I used to go out on the bayou, catching crawfish, turtles, whatever was biting. And after I'd caught enough or given up, I'd walk along the edge of the bayou, sneaking closer and closer until I was close enough to see this veranda, but far enough away that I could run like hell if anybody saw me. You used to sit out here all by yourself on summer nights. I always timed my fishing expeditions to coincide with the time you wandered onto the veranda."

He pointed to a big cypress tree close to where the marshy shoreline of the bayou began. "I watched you grow up peeking around that tree."

"You never told me that when we were..."

"Together? Maybe that's because we always had so little time, I preferred to spend it in your arms rather than waste it talking about the past. Besides, I stopped when I was twelve."

"Why?"

Jake looked out toward the bayou. "Your daddy saw me, and ran me off. Told me not to ever come back."

Annabelle's heart broke a little for the boy he had been. "Something else you never mentioned."

"Like I said, we were always short on time."

They fell silent, and when he turned to her, she sensed that he was about to ask the question she had been dreading. Regardless of the fact that he had told her he'd known the relationship was doomed from the start, that he didn't blame her, every instinct was telling her he still had to ask the question. He needed to ask.

"What happened to us, Anna?"

How could she tell him she hadn't been brave enough to cling to his love? That she had sacrificed not only his love, but her freedom. "You said it yourself. We were just kids."

"Looking back, I think I always expected it to end the way it did."

Her head snapped around. "What do you mean?"

"Just that I didn't have enough self-confidence to expect anything else. I think somewhere in the back of my mind was a small voice telling me I didn't deserve anything as fine and wonderful as you."

"Jake—"

"No. Wait. It took me years to realize that believing that message was what really cost me a future with you. I was my own worst enemy. I had been telling myself all along that one day you would wake up and realize we didn't belong together. One day you would wake up and say goodbye. When it happened, I told myself, 'See, you were right all along.'"

"But you weren't right," she blurted without thinking. "It wasn't you. It was me." Oh, God. What had she done? She had to explain her statement or face more questions. "I...I didn't have the courage to face being...poor,'' she lied. "I was weak. And I've lived with that shame for a long time.''

He walked over to where she sat, reached out a hand and stroked her cheek. "I told you. I don't blame you. And there's no reason for you to blame yourself. Anna, you were born into a life of money and tradition. You grew up surrounded by luxury. Of course you would be frightened at the prospect of walking away from all of that. You'd hardly be human if you weren't scared.''

"You make it sound so simple to put the past behind us. Some things aren't so easily dismissed.''

He took both her hands in his and pulled her to her feet. "What are you afraid of?''

"I...I... What makes you think I'm afraid?''

"Because when I hold you, kiss you, I feel your need, your yearning for more, and I'm not just talking about a physical relationship. I feel your need to be with me emotionally, as well, but just when I think you're about to let it happen, you pull back. Why?''

"Oh, Jake.''

"You're afraid of something. Anna, I know I asked before, but I have to be sure. Did Rowland abuse you in any way? Is that what this fear is about?''

"You mean did he hit me? No.''

"There are all kinds of abuse. Everything from a beating to simply being so cold, so unloving that the scars are every bit as deep as any physical blow.''

"I suppose, but Neal never deliberately hurt me.''

"Are you sure? Forgive me, but I already have a pretty good picture of your marriage through things Cade has said to Ty. He doesn't understand how his father can turn his back and walk away from him. Frankly, neither do I. Your ex-husband sounds like a first-class son of a bitch to me. He hasn't even called or written to Cade since you've been in Louisiana.''

"He cut us out of his life."

"And I'd be willing to bet it wasn't a recent thing."

"No. Our marriage started falling apart a couple of years ago. Neal just slowly turned away from us." Because he couldn't live with the truth, she thought. And as cruel as Neal had been at times, she didn't blame him.

"That's what I'm talking about. That kind of behavior is a form of abuse." He pulled her into his arms and held her. "I won't push you to talk about it, but I want you to know that when you're ready, I'll be here to listen. And when you're ready to trust again, I'll be here, too."

If only it were that easy, she thought. If only it were that simple. Just let him go on believing she was afraid because of Neal's coldness. Just keep living the lie, only with a new chapter. A new false front, this time to cover a lie of omission. If only she could.

"In the meantime..." He turned her in his arms, cupped her face in his hands and brushed his lips over hers. "I don't want you to think I'm all patience and wait-and-see. I want you, Anna."

She tried to tell herself the reason she didn't resist was that the kiss took her by surprise, but even she wasn't that good a liar. The instant his lips touched hers, she realized she had been waiting for this all night. Anticipating the stirring within her that started deep and spread. Spread quickly. She leaned forward, unable to stand even inches of distance between them. That unpredictable, always demanding hunger speared through her, and his name tumbled from her lips as she sought to bring him closer.

The soft, urgent sound of his name almost made him forget where they were. Almost snapped his control. Gently, he drew back. "Anna." His breathing was uneven and harsh-sounding in the night air. "Sweet, responsive. Anna. I told myself the touch and taste of you had always driven me insane because I'd been too young to control myself. I was wrong. You still drive me crazy."

When she swayed toward him, he stopped her. "And if I don't get out of here this minute, I'm going to let you drive me crazy. Hell, I'm going to beg you to." He stepped away from her, his hands shaking. "But there'll come a time when we don't have to worry about being on your father's veranda or anything else."

Flustered and a little shocked at her behavior, Annabelle didn't know what to say.

"I'll call you tomorrow," Jake said, his voice suddenly as shaky as his hands. With only a light touch on her shoulder, he led her to the back door and waited while she opened it and let herself inside.

"Good night," Anna whispered, and then he was gone.

ANNABELLE SPENT the entire next day in New Orleans. She visited Katherine Beaufort's shop, K & D's Antiques, and had lunch with Katherine and her delightful partner, Dionne. After purchasing several items in their shop, she turned her attention to the basic equipment for running a business in a high-tech world, even if it was a turn-of-the-century bed-and-breakfast. She purchased a pager and cellular phone and a fax machine in the name of her new business, Portier House Bed and Breakfast. She also ordered business cards. Then she shopped for some new clothes for Cade and a pair of shoes for herself, stretching her day into late afternoon.

Prolonging going home. Prolonging facing Jake.

She knew as surely as sunrise that there would be a message from him waiting for her when she got home. Just as she knew that ignoring it wouldn't do any good. So what did she think she was doing sipping a cold drink, resting on a bench just inside the entrance to Riverwalk mall? Collecting her thoughts? That didn't make sense, because every time she collected them, they were all about Jake. Was she trying to pretend she could handle the situation? Pretending was about all she could do. And every time she thought about pretending, she remembered how easy it would be to let Jake think she had been mistreated by Neal. How simple it would be to let his assumption continue to cover her sin to the point that even she might be able to forget. Might be able to start over.

With Jake.

Annabelle jabbed the straw into the crushed ice of her drink. All right, she admitted, at least now it was out in the open. There was no sin in wanting, was there? Probably. Especially the way she wanted Jake. So, what was wrong with a little healthy desire? Nothing, so long as desire was all she had to deal with. But, of course, it wasn't. No. What she was dealing with was loving Jake. The wanting was part of it, but the rest... The rest was all wrapped up around her heart's secret wishes. Those wishes she had held on to all these years, never expecting they would be more than wishes. But now they were more, or could be. And she had to decide what she was going to do about it.

She pitched the drink container into a trash receptacle and stomped out of the mall, heading back to her car. Instead of taking Interstate 10 to Slidell, she decided to take the causeway, even though it was the long way home. She told herself it was for the view, not another delaying tactic, but she hardly fooled herself.

As she drove along the ribbon of highway that stretched over the dark blue-green water of Lake Pontchartrain, she thought about the bizarre string of circumstances that had brought her to this time in her life. Cade's accident two years ago. Neal's rejection, however justified. The divorce. Moving back. Her path crossing Jake's. Cade and Ty's friendship. Coincidence?

She had tried to dismiss it as such. Even tried to tell herself that she could take the course of least resistance, just do nothing, and eventually, Jake would give up. She had tried to tell herself the fates were conspiring against her, but if they were conspiring, she knew now it was for, not against.

No, this wasn't coincidence, she thought, exiting the causeway and heading south on Interstate 12 into Bayou Beltane. This was her life. She was where she was for a reason. And the only reason she could see was that it was time for her to take control of her life in a way she never had before. Time for her to face the inevitable. Time to tell the truth. She had a responsibility to herself, Jake and Cade, and she could either run from that responsibility or face it.

It wouldn't be easy. She couldn't just blurt out the truth in one quick revelation. That might be the easiest way out for her, but too many lives would be affected. Timing was everything. She had to prepare Jake and Cade. And she didn't delude herself that once she told them everything, they would immediately forgive her. There would be pain. Lots of it, on all sides. All the reasons she had to avoid the truth were still there, but now she knew that her heart had led her back to her hometown, back to Jake and the love they had shared. And she prayed her heart would still be in one piece once she had revealed the truth.

Spanish moss dripped from trees along the road to Belle Terre, swaying like lacy fans in the breeze. As Annabelle pulled into the driveway, she saw her father's Town Car parked next to Drew's sporty Mercedes coupe. She took a deep breath and got out of her car. Her father would strongly oppose her decision to be honest about the past, and for that reason, she decided he would be the last to know.

She skirted the back door, knowing André was probably in full swing preparing for dinner, and came in through the French doors at the side of the house. The house was so quiet she might have thought it was empty if she hadn't seen the cars outside. Her father was probably in his study, and no telling where Drew was.

Crossing the parlor, she dropped her purchases on a sofa and picked up the phone on the end table. She would call Cade to see if he and Ty were finished working on their biology project and if he was ready to be picked up. As soon as she dialed the number, she realized she could have called him from her brand-new cellular phone and avoided a trip back into town. All this technology would take some getting used to.

Once she had spoken to Cade and told Mrs. Segal she would pick him up around eight o'clock, she lugged her purchases upstairs, thinking she might put her feet up for a while before dinner. She had just opened her bedroom door when she heard voices coming from her father's room at the other end of the long hall.

Drew and her daddy were arguing.

For a second she thought about ignoring them, then decided to play peacemaker if she could. She stepped into her room, deposited her bags on her bed and walked out into the hall. These arguments had been increasing lately. Her father had always been demanding, and Drew usually went along with his demands, but recently she'd noticed he was turning a deaf ear. Predictably, Philip was not pleased.

As she lifted her hand to knock on the door to her father's suite, she heard Drew say, "I can't believe you have the nerve to stand there and actually be proud of what you've done."

"Why wouldn't I be proud? I'm taking care of my family. I'm ensuring that the Delacroix name retains the prestige it has enjoyed for over a hundred years. What's wrong with that?"

"Family? How can you even use the word when you've just stabbed your own daughter in the back?"

Annabelle's hand stilled, then dropped to her side.

"Rubbish. I did nothing of the kind. I was protecting Annabelle and her future."

"By blocking her loan? By contacting your friends and making sure no one in St. Tammany Parish would loan her a nickel to buy that house?"

Annabelle couldn't believe what she was hearing. Surely there must be some mistake, but dread crept up her spine like a spider.

"Running a bed-and-breakfast. What kind of career is that for the daughter of a state senator? Besides, it's just a passing fancy. I know Annabelle. Once she gets over this, she'll settle down."

"And do exactly what you want her to do, right?"

Before her father could answer, she opened the door.

"Annabelle!" Philip smiled and adjusted his bow tie. "I was hoping to have the pleasure of your company for dinner. Did you just get home this minute?"

She walked straight over to where they stood. "No. I've been here long enough." Then she glanced at her brother. "Drew, would you mind leaving Daddy and me alone?"

He grinned. "You got it."

When he had closed the door behind him, she turned to her father.

Philip heaved a theatrical sigh. "I suppose you overheard our conversation, and now you're upset with me."

Annabelle looked at the man who had sired her as if she were seeing a perfect stranger. But her shock was quickly replaced by a wave of anger so strong it blurred her vision for a moment. Her hands doubled into fists at her sides and it took every ounce of willpower she possessed, and some she didn't even know she had, not to slap him.

"Upset?" she whispered, her voice shaking.

"You know, I've been thinking that this old house needs a face-lift. How would you like to redecorate Belle Terre? You could turn it into even more of a showplace than it already is." Casually, as though he had nothing more pressing to deal with, Philip strolled over to an antique secretary and flipped through some papers. "You can't go hog-wild, of course, but within reason, money's no object. When you're done, we'll throw a big party."

His indifference cooled her rage as nothing else could have. She refused to give him the upper hand in this situation. Every instinct she had was screaming that what she'd overhead was true, yet she needed to have him admit the truth to her. Face-to-face.

"Turn around," she told him in a strong, clear voice.

"Pardon me?"

"Turn around and look at me. I want the truth. Did you stop my loan requests?"

"Annabelle—"

"All I want is a simple yes or no."

"If you'll just simmer down—"

"Tell me, damn it!"

Philip cleared his throat. "Yes," he said, not a bit of remorse in his voice. "I most certainly did."

CHAPTER TEN

SHE HATED HIM. At that moment she actually hated her father. Her heart struggled with that hate while her mind reeled with the sheer incredulity of what he'd done. He had played around with her life as if it were a chess piece in some larger game he was playing for his own enjoyment. Suddenly Joanna's words came back to her.

You don't know him or what he's capable of...power broker...manipulator...incredibly selfish...ruthless.

"Now, Annabelle—"

"Don't." She held up both her hands as if to protect herself from more of his stinging words. "Don't insult my intelligence by trying to tell me everything you've done was for my own good. Everything you do is for the good of Philip Delacroix. And no one else."

"I won't have you speak to me like that."

"And I won't have you running my life. You don't have the faintest idea of who I am or what I want. And in the last few minutes it's become painfully clear to me that you don't care."

"That's not true. I've always cared about you."

"Like when you wanted me to have an abortion? When you packaged me up and married me off to the son of one of your political cronies when I was in love with Jake?"

"Ah, that's where all this rebellion comes from. Jake Trahan. I should have known."

"He has nothing to do with this."

"Doesn't he? You were fine until he walked back into the picture."

"Fine? You mean fine, according to your standards. You mean fine, as in safely tucked away in Florida. Only it wasn't so safe, was it, Daddy? Our little secret was in danger of exposure. I wouldn't be surprised if the only reason you wanted me back in Bayou Beltane was so that you could keep an eye on me. Make sure I didn't spill the beans and spoil your precious reputation, tarnish the Delacroix name."

She stopped, paling at the look in his eyes. "Oh, my God. It's true. I only half believed it when I said it, but now I can see that it's true. You had to have me close to make sure I kept my mouth shut, didn't you?"

"That's the most ludicrous thing I've ever heard."

"I haven't even gotten started. No, wait. That's not true. I've finished. Completely. Totally. As of this minute, you don't have to concern yourself with me anymore. I'm getting out of this house, and out of your life." She turned and headed for the door.

"And what about Cade? Is he included in this little temper tantrum?"

She pivoted and faced him. "Listen very carefully, Daddy, because this is the only time I intend to say this. Cade is my son. My son." She pointed to herself. "I will see that he has everything he needs."

"And just how do you propose to accomplish that when you don't have an income and no prospects of one?"

Annabelle smiled. "Oh, but I do."

"What do you mean?"

She was enjoying this. Perhaps a little too much. "I have my loan. The papers are signed. It's a done deal."

His mouth fell open, but only for a half a second. Then his gaze narrowed. "Where? You might as well tell me. I'll find out, anyway."

"Bayou Bank and Trust. And if you want to threaten the bank president or call in a marker, fine. I already had other sources ready to invest when the bank decided to give me the loan. So you see, Daddy, your nasty little trick was wasted effort."

"You won't like living without servants and in such splendor," Philip pronounced, as if that were the only reason for living.

"Right now a cardboard box underneath an overpass sounds better than spending one more night in the same house with you." And she turned and walked away.

HALF AN HOUR LATER she had packed a bag for Cade and one for herself and was driving away from Belle Terre just as dusk gathered. There was only one person Annabelle knew who would understand, and she punched Joanna's number into her cell phone.

"Hello?"

"Joanna, it's Annabelle."

"Annie, how are you?"

"Fine. Listen, I hate to ask, but do you think you could put Cade and me up for tonight? I know it's an inconvenience, but—"

"You've moved out?"

"Yes."

There was a pause, then Joanna said, "I see."

"Better than I did up until now, apparently. I'll tell you about it when I see you."

"Of course you and Cade are welcome. We'll be a

little crowded, but the more the merrier. When can I expect you?"

"Is now too soon?"

Joanna laughed. "Now is perfect. I'll make up the guest room. See you in a few minutes."

"Thanks," Annabelle said, and hung up. She immediately punched in the number to Jake's house.

"Hello again, Mrs. Segal. Annabelle Rowland. Could I speak with my son?"

"Hey, Mom," Cade said when he came to the phone.

"Listen, pal. We've got a bit of a problem. You and I have moved out of Belle Terre as of tonight. Your aunt—"

"We did what?"

"Moved out."

"You're not kiddin' me, are you? You wouldn't do that to a poor little kid, would ya?"

"Poor little kid, my foot. Seriously, I've made it clear to your granddaddy that we're not coming back."

"Who wants to?"

"Well, I'll have to go back to pack up the rest of our things, otherwise, we're gone. Your aunt Joanna has offered us a place to sleep tonight, but I promise that tomorrow I'll find us something temporary until the house is finished."

"Can't I stay here?"

She could hear muffled voices in the background as if Cade had put his hand over the phone and was talking to Ty or Mrs. Segal. Sure enough, Cade said, "Mrs. Segal said it was all right with her, but she has to check with the chief."

Annabelle hesitated, then gave in. "If it's okay with

Jake, then fine. What about school tomorrow? Is Ty going?''

"Yeah, he's doing great."

"That's wonderful. Oh, by the way, I packed some things for you and I'll bring them over as soon as Jake gives his official okay. And I need to give you a number where you can reach me anytime." She recited the number. "It's for my new cell phone."

"No kiddin'? A cell phone. Cool."

"And I've got a pager."

"All right, Mom. Movin' on up."

"Yeah, well, we'll see how far and how fast I'm moving. It isn't going to be easy from here on in."

"I know, but don't worry, Mom. We'll make it."

And they would, she realized. Whatever it took, they would make it.

"Okay, pal. Call me and let me know if Jake agrees to the sleepover."

When she hung up from talking to Cade, Annabelle felt better than she had in ages. Free. The feeling was exhilarating. She felt like a kid out on her own for the first time, and then she realized that's exactly what she was. She had gone from her daddy's house into marriage with Neal, then from divorce back into her father's house again. She'd never really been on her own.

"Well, you are now," she said, pulling into her sister's driveway.

Joanna came out to greet her, and together they walked back into the house. "I'm so glad you called," she told Annabelle.

"I can't thank you enough for taking us in." She glanced around. "Where's Nikki?"

"Upstairs keeping her computer company. I can't tell you what weight has been lifted from my shoulders now that she's stopped seeing Steven Boudreaux! I was really sweating that one. How lucky you are that Cade hasn't started dating yet."

Annabelle rolled her eyes. "As if I don't have enough on my plate."

"Where is Cade, by the way?"

"He's spending the night with Ty Trahan, I think."

"You think?"

"We're waiting for confirmation from Jake."

Joanna glanced out her living room window and noticed a car pull up. She went over to the window and peered out. "Well, either he's delivering the confirmation in person, or we're being arrested."

"What?"

"Jake Trahan is coming up the walk," Joanna explained just about the time that the doorbell rang. She opened the door. "Good evening, Chief."

"Mrs. Gideon. I, uh, I'm looking for Annabelle—"

"Here, Jake," she said, stepping into view. "I didn't expect you to give me an answer in person."

"I was on a call a couple of streets over, so when Ty phoned, I decided to come by."

"Come on in, Chief," Joanna told him. "I was just about to make a pot of coffee. Could I interest you in a cup?"

"No, thanks."

"All right. I'll be back in a minute, Annie."

As Joanna was leaving the room, Annabelle asked, "Is there a problem with Cade staying at your house tonight?"

"No. But when Ty called, he mentioned that you had moved out of Belle Terre. Is that true?"

"Absolutely."

Jake stepped closer and reached out to take her hand. "Are you okay?"

She nodded, squeezing his fingers.

"Anything I can do?"

"No. Tomorrow I'm going to find a place to stay until the house is fit for us to occupy. Everything else—" she shrugged "—I'll just have to play by ear."

"You know if there's anything you need, all you have to do is call me."

"I know, and I appreciate it. Are you sure having an extra teenager in the house isn't more than you bargained for?"

"Who, Cade? He's a great kid. You've done a terrific job of raising him, Anna. Seriously, you can be proud of him."

Though his words swelled her heart with pride, Annabelle wasn't sure she could handle any more emotion after the day she'd had. She offered him a watery smile. "Thanks."

"You sure you're okay?"

"I'm fine. Really."

He looked hesitant, then nodded. "Well, then I guess I better get home and check on the bald bunch. Walk me to my car?"

"Joanna," she called out, picking up the bag she had packed for Cade. "I'm going to walk out with Jake. I'll be right back."

"Fine. See you, Chief," Joanna said from the kitchen.

"Goodbye, Mrs. Gideon."

Once outside, Jake pulled her into his arms. "I've been wanting to do this all day."

She rested her head on his chest, savoring the sweetness of being in his arms. "Have you?" She sighed.

"Mmm, this feels good. I'm glad you put in a personal appearance." The thought crossed her mind that they were standing on her sister's front lawn, embracing for the world to see, but she didn't care.

"Yeah. Me, too. Anna?"

"Hmm?"

"You didn't have a fight with your brother, did you? Word around town is that Drew can get a little belligerent when he's had a few drinks."

She raised her head and looked up at him. "No. I didn't fight with Drew. I fought with my father." When he started to speak, she put her finger against his mouth. "Not tonight. I'll tell you about it, but not tonight."

"If you say so." He kissed her finger. "Can I call you here tomorrow?"

"I bought a cellular phone today. From now on, you can reach me day or night."

"Day or night, huh?" Jake grinned. "I like the sound of that. I like the idea that I can get in touch with you anywhere, anytime."

They walked to her car so she could give him the cell phone number. Annabelle set Cade's bag down and reached through the open driver's side window to pick up the phone. With a gentle tug, Jake urged her to step back. He opened the back door. "Get in."

"But—"

"Scoot over," he said as her fanny barely touched the upholstery.

Before she realized his intent, he was beside her, drawing her into his arms. "There's something else I've been wanting to do all day."

His mouth was on hers before she could take a breath, and for the life of her she couldn't remember all the reasons why this was a bad idea. But then, how bad could anything be that felt so good? *Good?* Such a mundane word could never describe the blood rushing through her veins like a river of fire, or the complexity of the emotions swirling through her as Jake kissed her practically senseless.

"Whoa," she whispered when he finally ended the kiss.

"You got that right." He kissed her cheek, her earlobe and her neck, deliberately avoiding her lips. "You know, it might look bad for the chief of police to be caught making out in the back seat of a car, but I'll chance it if you will."

Annabelle gave a soft, breathy laugh. "Aren't we a little old for back seats?"

He drew back and looked into her eyes. "You're right. We did that, didn't we."

"Yes." The night of her seventeenth birthday, in fact. Jake had borrowed a friend's car and they had driven to the Pearl River and parked. He'd found a secluded spot and they had stayed until the wee hours of the morning. It was a glorious time.

And she almost certain it was the night Cade was conceived.

"Yes," she said. "We did."

"Remember that abandoned boathouse on the other side of the lake? That makeshift bed?"

"I remember everything."

"I wouldn't trade those memories." He kissed her lips. "But we're not teenagers anymore, and we don't have to meet in secret. The next time I make love to you, I want it to be in a bed. And I want us to have all night to enjoy each other."

Annabelle longed to tell him how much she wanted

the same thing, but it might never happen, would never happen when she told him the truth.

He rested his forehead on hers. "But for now, I suppose I should do the responsible thing and go home."

"I suppose," she whispered as his mouth came down on hers again for one last taste.

She was still smiling when she walked back into Joanna's house ten minutes later.

"I think your coffee's cold," Joanna said as Annabelle joined her in the living room.

She took a sip and shrugged. "It'll do."

"Want to tell me what happened?" Her dismay must have been obvious, because Joanna grinned. "Not with Jake. I'm talking about why you left Belle Terre."

"There's very little to tell, really. Daddy attempted to stop my loan and—"

"You're sure?"

She took a deep breath. "As you suspected, he went to the bank and the other lending institutions I had contacted and threw his weight around to stop the loan."

"How did you find out?"

"I overheard Daddy and Drew arguing about it. When I walked in and asked him point blank, he said yes."

"I'm sorry, Annie."

"You warned me."

"I know, but I didn't want you to find out like this."

"Joanna, I looked into his eyes when I asked him, and it was like looking into the eyes of a stranger. You were right. I don't know my own father. And what's more, I don't want to know him."

"Be careful, Annie."

"Careful?"

"Don't expect Daddy to give up and bow out gracefully."

"I've moved out, and there's nothing he can do about it."

Joanna frowned. "I'm just saying that he will use every means at his disposal to stop you if he can. If he can't..."

"What?"

"Then he may try to hurt you."

"You mean more than he already has?"

Joanna was silent a moment. "He hates to lose. And he also isn't above revenge, so just be careful. He's convinced you're making a mistake, and he's also convinced that he knows what's best for you, better than you do."

"I think that's the greatest insult of all. He really thinks I don't have enough brains to get along without him. Well, he's wrong."

"Of course he is. He was wrong about me. And you. And he's wrong about Drew."

"Drew?"

"He'll see it for himself sooner or later. He has to."

"I don't know. So far, he hasn't been any better at standing up to Daddy than I have. But I hope you're right, for Drew's sake."

"Well, right now I want to help you and Cade get squared away. Drew's a big boy. He can take care of himself."

"The first thing I have to do is find a place to live."

Joanna set her coffee mug on the table next to her chair. "Correct me if I'm wrong, but aren't you buying a house?"

"Yes, but the closing isn't until next week."

"So? You've got your loan. Call Bud Snider and tell him you want to close on the house this week."

"Can I do that?"

"Annie, you're the first person to even look at that house in over eight months. Trust me, they'll do whatever it takes to accommodate you."

"But what good will that do? There's tons of work to be done."

"In every room?"

"No. Actually, the downstairs is in good shape. It's only the upstairs that needs work due to a leaky roof."

"So, live downstairs."

"Live downstairs," Annabelle repeated, the idea simmering in her head. "Cade and I *could* live downstairs while the renovations are going on. That way I could keep an eye on their progress, and not have to find a temporary place. I could get some of my furniture out of storage. Just leave the rest until I'm ready." She looked at her sister. "Thank you. You're unbelievably organized."

Joanna shrugged. "Can't seem to live any other way." She rose with her coffee cup in hand. "Want a refill?"

"Sure." Annabelle followed her into the kitchen.

"My logic drives Nikki insane."

"It's also part of what makes you such an excellent lawyer. No wonder you and Shelby get along so well. You're like two peas in a pod."

Joanna laughed. "Oh, no. Shelby's methodical, all right, but she's also so tenacious she scares the hell out of me sometimes. She's taken that comment you made about a mother wanting to make sure her child wouldn't be around someone with a drug or alcohol problem and applied it to the custody case she's working on. She's even roped Lucas Henderson into helping her.''

"Lucas Henderson? Our cousin Marie's husband?''

"Uh-huh. They're playing Holmes and Watson over this case of Shelby's. Lord only knows where it will all end.'' She reached for the coffeepot.

"Well, all I know is that your wonderfully logical and highly organized brain has provided me with a way to kill two birds with one stone, so to speak. I wasn't looking forward to living out of a suitcase.''

"My pleasure. And until you get everything set up, you and Cade are welcome to stay here.''

THE FOLLOWING DAY was a whirlwind of activity. Joanna had been right. Bud Snider was more than willing to push the paperwork through, particularly since the lending institution was right there in Bayou Beltane and Annabelle was paying cash. In four days Portier House would be hers. In the meantime, there were things like carpenters, building permits and a million other details to attend to.

Jake called and invited her out to dinner that night, but by the time seven o'clock rolled around she had to cancel. She was totally exhausted, but happy. Even Cade didn't seem to mind having to sleep on Joanna's couch, knowing it was temporary.

By week's end, the Portier House was hers. As she walked out of the title company's offices, she couldn't remember when she had felt so happy since the day Cade was born. Feeling a glow all the way to her toes, she simply stood there for a moment, enjoying her happiness. She waved as Jake pulled up in his cruiser, parked and got out.

"From the smile on your face, I'd guess you're a proud homeowner."

"Oh, Jake," she said. "It's wonderful."

"So wonderful you deserve a celebration. How about you, me, Cade and Ty all going out to dinner?"

"Did you forget about the biology field trip this afternoon? The bus picks up the whole class around three o'clock, and with the trip to the laboratory and the lecture at Tulane, they won't be back until almost nine tonight."

Jake smiled. "I'd forgotten, but I can't say I'm disappointed. That means we can celebrate alone. How about dinner in Covington?"

"We'll have to make it early in order to be back in time to pick up the boys."

"How about six? Or earlier if you can make it."

"That's fine. I have several errands I have to accomplish, but other than that, I'm all yours."

His smiled widened. "I'm going to hold you to that," he said. "See you at six."

When Jake drove away, Annabelle walked to her car, still grinning. She intended to spend tonight in her very own home. When she'd told her sister about her idea to camp out until the few pieces of furniture she'd had removed from storage arrived the next afternoon, Joanna hadn't understood. Why not just wait? But Annabelle didn't want to wait. Okay, so camping out in an empty house wasn't exactly the norm. But the "norm" for her life had pretty much been up for grabs the last few months. Maybe it was eccentric. But it was also going to be fun. Beds or no beds, she and Cade were spending the night in their new home.

Annabelle ran her local errands, then made a flying trip to the Wal-Mart store in Slidell to purchase a couple of sleeping bags, a lantern and two folding chairs, then headed back to Bayou Beltane. As she pulled up in front of the house, a feeling of pride and accomplishment almost overwhelmed her. They were still a long way off from opening the doors to guests, but it *would* happen. When she turned the key in the lock, the door seemed to waiver, and she realized she was seeing it through tears of joy. She went inside and stood in the center of the wide foyer for long minutes, basking in sheer pleasure at being in her own home. Then she walked to the back of the house and opened the door to what would be her bedroom. Sunlight filtered through the admittedly dirty windows, but she didn't care. So much promise for the future was in this house. So much—

"Annabelle?"

She whirled around to find her father standing in the hall. Damn, she'd left that door unlocked again. For a heartbeat she considered telling him to leave, then changed her mind. Demanding that he leave would only make matters worse, and there was nothing to be gained by more insults and angry words. She was hurt and disappointed by his reprehensible behavior, but she had no intention of lowering herself to his level. She would simply try to make the best of an uncomfortable situation.

"Hello, Daddy," she said, her tone cool.

Philip glanced around the hall then strolled back to the foyer, and for a moment she thought he had decided to leave. She walked back to the front of the house to join him.

"Was there something you wanted to see me about, Daddy?"

"I came to take you home."

"This is my home."

"Ridiculous. This isn't a home. Look around you. It's...crude."

"It's still a little rough around the edges, but as of today—" she tossed the key up into the air and caught it "—it's all mine."

"I'm sure your sister has promoted this whole affair. She'd like nothing better than to use you to get back at me."

"Joanna doesn't want to do any such thing. Neither do I. All I want is to live my life the way I choose."

"Here." He glanced around, clearly disgusted.

"Yes. Here. Now, if you'll excuse me, Daddy, I have—"

"Are you dismissing me?"

"No. I'm simply trying to tell you that I'm busy. When the house is in better shape, perhaps you'd like to come back and—"

"Come back? I hardly think so." He sighed and rubbed the bridge of his nose. "If it's an apology you want, then fine."

"And if that's your idea of an apology, I'll pass."

"Annabelle," he said sharply. "I insist you stop this nonsense and come back to Belle Terre."

She didn't want this showdown, but it was clear to her now there was no other way her father was going to be convinced that she meant what she said. Maybe it was just as well, she decided. Lord knew, she had avoided this day for years.

"I'm not coming back to live at Belle Terre. Ever."

Philip pursed his lips and his eyes took on that hard, cold look that had been known to wither at twenty paces. She'd been frightened by it all her life. But no more.

"You actually think," he said, his drawl accentuating the word, *actually*, "you can make a living renting rooms?"

"That's an oversimplification of my planned business, but yes."

"I will never understand why you would prefer this to Belle Terre."

"I know you can't. That's the problem."

"Oh," he huffed. "You're making too much of what happened, Annabelle. I know your feelings were hurt, but if this is your idea of revenge—"

"This is not about revenge or rebellion or any other damn thing. And once and for all, it's not about *you*. It's about what I want. What I need to be happy. Sixteen years ago I let you convince me that you knew me better than I knew myself, and maybe there was some truth to that back then. But not anymore."

His gaze flicked over her. "And just where do you think you'd be if I hadn't taken control of that situation sixteen years ago?"

Annabelle looked him straight in the eye. "Happy. I'd be with the man I love, and Cade would be with his real father. Look, Daddy, I can't change the past. I'm going to have enough trouble just dealing with the future, but my point is that it's *my* future, and Cade's."

"You force me to do something I had hoped never to do," Philip said. "I don't approve of what you're doing, and unless you're willing to change your mind, I have serious doubts about any financial support that might be coming to you upon my death."

"Your what?"

"I think you heard me clearly enough."

"So, unless I clean up my act, I'm out of the will, is that it?"

"I didn't exactly say that."

"The hell you didn't."

"Don't curse, Annabelle, it's very unladylike."

She told him what he could do with "unladylike," and she used a decidedly unladylike word to do it. Her vocabulary of profanity wasn't very extensive, but she made her point.

"Keep your money," she told him. "I've never needed luxury."

"But I assume you'll need grocery money, and money to pay the mortgage. What kind of business reputation would you have if it were to get out that you were sleeping with the chief of police?"

"I'm not, and you know it."

He shrugged. "People believe what they want to believe."

With a ragged sigh, Annabelle folded her arms over her chest. He was deliberately hurting her. Her own father was deliberately hurting her. She struggled past the pain to the anger. It was all she had.

"You won't open your mouth about the past, because you don't want the precious Delacroix name tarnished. Careful, Daddy, you might wind up tarred with the same brush you use on me."

Philip walked past her into the library. "I wouldn't necessarily have to tell everyone," he said, and for a moment she thought his voice sounded like the hiss of a snake. He cast a bored glance around the room, delaying what he was about to say for greater effect. "Just Jake...and Cade. How do you think Cade would feel about you if he knew?"

Somewhere in the back of her mind she had known this was where he was heading, but it still made her sick to her stomach. She took a deep breath.

"Well, we're finally down to the nitty-gritty. Let's just review for a moment, shall we? You insult my home, offer a half-assed apology, impugn my ability to earn a decent living, insinuate I'm out for revenge, then try to manipulate me with guilt. Then we have the threats. First, I'm out of the will. Then you threaten to grind me up in the gossip mill. And finally, you threaten me with the truth."

Annabelle ran out of breath and patience at the same time. She put one hand on her hip and shoved a wave of hair back from her face with the other. "I'll save you the trouble. I intend to tell Cade and Jake myself."

For an instant Philip's nostrils flared and his eyes sparked with...she wasn't certain, but she thought it was hate. He adjusted his bow tie, squared his shoulders and walked past her and out of the house without another word.

As she watched him go, Joanna's words echoed in her mind.

Be careful, Annie. Don't expect Daddy to bow out gracefully.

CHAPTER ELEVEN

ANNABELLE TRIED TO BLOT her father's visit from her mind, but it wasn't easy. She hadn't wanted a confrontation and wished she had simply told him to leave. On second thought, if she were honest with herself, the confrontation had been coming for a long time, and maybe, secretly, she *had* wanted it. Maybe this was the confrontation they should have had sixteen years ago. In any case, each knew where the other stood now.

Determined to shake off the gloom of the past few minutes, she drove her car around to the back and unloaded the sleeping bags, along with a box of cleaning supplies and a change of clothes. She slipped into an old, ratty pair of jeans and a T-shirt, then, armed with rags and a bottle of finishing restorative, went to tackle the wood paneling in the library. Starting with the mantel and the trim around the fireplace, Annabelle worked to clean and restore the parched wood until her arms throbbed and her back ached. But it was worth the effort when she stepped back to view her handiwork. The oak gleamed with a rich luster, making the hand-carved molding and the trim stand out handsomely. Despite her sore muscles, she jumped right back into the job. The more she did, the better the room looked, and the more she wanted to do. She became obsessed with seeing the room completed. So much so that she lost

all track of time as she worked, and when her cell
phone rang, it startled her.

"Hello?"

"Hi there," Jake said. "Where are you?"

"At the house."

"I'm calling about dinner."

"Oh..." She glanced at her watch, only to realize
she had taken it off when she changed clothes. "What
time is it?"

"Six."

"Oh, good grief. I'm sorry. I got so involved in
working on the library. I had no idea what time it was.
Listen, I'll run to Joanna's, shower and be ready in
thirty minutes."

"No, wait. I hate to do this, but I'm afraid we'll
have to reschedule dinner. I'm going to be tied up for
forty-five minutes to an hour. How about a rain
check?"

"Sure."

"But we still need to eat, so how about I pick you
up when I'm done and we'll grab a couple of burgers
before we get the boys. I'll call you as soon as I'm
finished, okay?"

"Sounds fine."

After she hung up, Annabelle glanced around the
foyer. She still had time to do one wall, she decided,
then a quick shower and she'd be ready for Jake.

SHOWERED, SHAVED and looking forward to some time
with Anna, Jake dialed Joanna's number. After three
rings the answering machine picked up. He left a message, but when he hung up, he decided to try Anna's
cellular number. It rang and rang and rang. He tried
the number again, making sure he had dialed it cor-

rectly. Again, there was no answer, and no recording indicating she had turned the phone off. Where was she?

He waited about five minutes, then tried the cell phone again. Still no answer. Five more very impatient minutes passed. He redialed her sister's number, and this time Joanna answered.

"Hello?"

"Mrs. Gideon, this is Jake Trahan. Could I speak to Annabelle?"

"She's...not here."

"Where is she?"

"At the—her house. She and Cade are sleeping there tonight."

"What?"

"They're camping out."

Three minutes later he was in his car, headed for the Portier House.

The lights were on in the library when he pulled up, but he didn't see Anna's car.

Or any sign of Anna.

Out of habit, he immediately went into cop mode, glancing around as he walked to the front door and rang the bell. No answer had him trying the lock, then he doubled up his fist and pounded on the door.

"Anna!" Oh, Lord, where was she? If anything had happened to her... "Anna, are you in there?" He could hear a noise inside, someone moving around, but still there was no answer. Half a heartbeat before he was ready to kick in the door, it opened.

"Jake!"

He pushed her inside and slammed the door. "Where have you been? And why the hell didn't you answer me? Do you realize I was just about to kick in your door?''

"I—I was taking a shower."

"I thought you were going to Joanna's to shower," Jake stormed.

"I was, until I realized I could just as easily do it here." She pulled the lapels of her robe together. "I only just this minute came to the front of the house and...Jake, you're shaking."

"Damn right I'm shaking. But I should be shaking you. Do you have any idea how scared I was? I imagined all kinds of things that might have happened to you, and in my line of work, that's a lot. Don't ever—" he gripped her shoulders and literally lifted her off her feet "— ever do that again." He brought his mouth down hard on hers, his intent clear. Possession. Mate claiming mate.

For an instant Annabelle staggered under the assault, then she recovered enough to clutch his shirt and hang on, because she was positive the earth had been jerked out from beneath her feet. She felt as if she were suspended in a wind tunnel, the air whipping around her, tugging at her clothes, her hair. Only Jake had the ability to make her feel this way. To need this way. God, how could she have forgotten how wonderful passion could be? When she could breathe again, she looked into his eyes, dark with possession and his own need.

"Jake, I'm—"

"God, Anna, I'm sorry." He set her on her feet again. "I don't know what came over me. When I saw you standing there...I just had to touch you. I had to know you were all right."

"I'm...fine," she whispered, her heart drumming

against her rib cage. Actually she was better than fine, considering the way he'd kissed her.

In the process of lifting her up, Jake inadvertently forced her robe to gap. The tempting swell of her breasts drew his gaze, and a jolt of desire shot through him.

"I didn't see your car...didn't know if you were in here."

"It's parked in the back."

"Your, uh... " He took a deep breath in an attempt to steady himself. "Your sister said your were staying here tonight?"

"Yes." She could see his eyes, still dark with need, and she remembered when she had seen that look, learned what it meant. He had introduced her to the taste and texture of passion with that look.

"I don't think that's a good idea."

It took her a second to realize what he was talking about. "What do you mean?" The last thing she needed right now was another man telling her what to do.

"I don't think you should stay here tonight."

From the intoxicating joy of closing the deal on the house to the anguish of her father's visit, plus the bone-melting effect of his kiss a moment ago, she felt as if her day had been one long emotional roller coaster ride. His comment, no matter how well-intentioned, was more than she could handle. She had reached her limit, and Jake had the misfortune to be the last in line.

"Too bad."

Her uncharacteristically clipped response took him by surprise. "What? What did you say?" But he was asking her retreating back. Quickly, he followed her into the library. "What did you just say?"

"Too bad. My son and I are sleeping in our new home tonight, and if you don't like it, that's tough. It's none of your damn business."

He glanced at the two lawn chairs, a cooler and the two sleeping bags lying on the floor near the fireplace. "You're going to sleep on those?"

"I told you, it's none of your business."

"Anna—"

"Save it, Jake. I'm not in the mood for another domineering man."

"Domineering?"

"You heard me." She sliced the air with her hand. "I've had it." All the passion he had so quickly tapped a moment ago seethed inside her, along with the lingering pain of her encounter with her father. Both needed release. "I'm not taking any more orders from anybody."

"But I didn't—"

"I'm going to live my life my way, do you hear? My way. And no one—not my father, not even you—is ever going to make decisions for me again."

"Anna."

"And I don't give a damn whether you like it or not."

"Anna."

"What?" she snapped.

"I'm not trying to tell you anything except that I'm concerned about your safety. I think you would be wiser to wait until some sort of security system is installed before you stay here, that's all."

His calm voice and caring words took the starch out of her temper. "Jake, I'm sorry. I..."

"It's okay." He put a hand on her shoulder. "You must've had one helluva day to be so uptight."

She glanced up at him. "A real bitch, if you'll pardon the language."

He drew her to him and she went willingly into his embrace. "Want to tell me about it?"

Annabelle sighed, calmer now, and slowly filled him in on what had happened. When she finished, he looked down into her eyes. "Why didn't you tell me any of this before now?"

"There's nothing you could have done. Once Philip Delacroix makes up his mind, it's etched in stone. At least as far as he's concerned. Never mind that whoever he's manipulating may have feelings or dreams. If they conflict with his, then pitch 'em, they're not important, anyway," she said. She could feel herself building up another head of steam. "When I think about all the times I've allowed him to rearrange my life, and never even made a whimper, because I thought whatever he did, he did out of love, it makes me sick to my stomach."

"Nobody blames you for trusting your father."

"I blame myself. If I hadn't let him manipulate me at every turn, you and I would have eloped the way we planned to, and…"

"What do you mean?"

"Nothing." She sighed, cowardice rearing its ugly head. "He's not your father, so it's not your problem."

"Haven't you figured out by now that whatever happens to you concerns me? Don't you understand how much I—"

"Yes, and I appreciate your concern, but—"

"You didn't let me finish. Everything about you concerns me because I love you. I've always loved you. And I'll go on loving you until my dying day. That doesn't mean I own you, or that I have any right to tell you what to do.'' In a tenderly familiar gesture he slipped his hand to the nape of her neck and drew her closer. ''All I want, all I've ever wanted, is to love you.'' He dipped his head and stroked her parted lips with his. ''Let me love you, Anna.''

This was no good, and too good, she thought, even as she melted in his arms. She could let him love her so easily, it was frightening. It would be unfair, it would be wrong, and her guilt insisted she recognize that. But when he took the kiss deeper, almost stealing her breath away, all she could think about was how right it felt to be in his arms. How long she had waited for him to love her.

His mouth moved over hers in an endless kiss, rife with passion, longing, hope and a million other sensations. When they finally came up for air, they were both trembling with need.

Annabelle tried to clear her head from the drugging effects of his kisses, but even if her mind had cooperated, her body refused. She shivered, desire singing through her blood, making it race with anticipation.

''Anna, Anna, Anna.'' He chanted her name as he bestowed kisses on her mouth then her neck and back again. ''I need you.''

She should beg him to stop. Have that much courage at least, she told herself, but it was useless. She wasn't going to beg him, unless it was for more.

''Yes,'' she whispered.

Jake let his hands coast down over her shoulders. ''I want you…but not like this. Not here. You deserve better.''

She should have been glad to hear the voice of reason; instead she almost panicked that he *wouldn't* make love to her. ''Yes. Here. Now.''

"But I promised the next time we made love it would be in a bed, and we'd have all night."

Her body moved restlessly against his. "Please," she said. "Haven't we waited long enough?"

The "please" undid him.

He scooped her into his arms, crossed to the fireplace and lowered her to stand beside one of the sleeping bags. When he started to pull away, she grabbed his sleeve.

"Where are you going?"

"The lights." In three strides he was across the floor to the light switch, and the room was plunged into semidarkness, leaving only the pale light from a silvery half moon for illumination. Then he was back. "I'd give anything to be able to see you in full light, but there are no drapes on these windows," he reminded her.

"Maybe it's just as well. I don't have the body of a seventeen-year-old anymore."

"No. You have the body of a woman. A beautiful woman."

He put his hands on her throat, then slowly slid them down the lapel of his robe to the sash knotted at her waist. With minimal effort the knot gave way. Then, just as slowly, he moved his hands back up along the now slack lapels until he reached the valley between her breasts. He parted the robe, pushing it from her shoulders, until it slid down her body, hitting the hard-wood floor with barely a sound.

"Oh, Anna," he said, his voice husky. "I've dreamed of seeing you like this so many times, but my dreams don't even compare to reality." When he reached out a trembling hand to caress her breasts, she sighed. "Soft. So soft," he said, cupping her fullness.

Sixteen years vanished with his touch. She was young again, his again, and nothing else mattered. She had never felt so cherished. So immersed in desire. It swirled around her, through her, like smoke around a blazing fire. Fire inside and out. She pressed against the palm of his hand then slowly moved back and forth until her nipples hardened, sending a streamer of need spiraling downward until she was moist with need.

Then he leaned her back just far enough for his mouth to cover the soft swell of her breast. When he teased the erect nipple, a moan of pleasure rose from deep within her.

The sound shot through Jake like an arrow, leaving a burning trail in its wake. He wanted to go slow, to be tender, but the desire he felt threatened to overwhelm him. Even as he lowered her to the sleeping bag and tore off his clothes, he tried to temper the rage of passion that gripped him. He stretched out beside her, stroking his hands over her velvety skin. When he felt her quiver beneath his touch, it almost snapped his control.

"I want to touch you," she whispered, rolling on her side. She ran her hand over his arm, his shoulder. So much power. So much heat. Then her fingers stroked his neck, skimmed along his jaw to his lips. "I love your mouth. So sexy."

Now it was Jake's turn to groan. He captured her hand and kissed her palm. "Yours drives me crazy. It always did."

"Let's not compare tonight to the past. There's only now." She moved closer, lifting her leg over his.

"Only now," he said, his hand sliding down her body until he found her soft heat. He stroked, driving her higher and higher. She pressed her hips forward, seeking more, needing more, until she gasped with her first shuddering release. Wave upon wave swept through her in a seemingly endless climax. When at last she was nearly limp, he relented only long enough to capture her hips and pull her flush against him.

They were flesh to flesh, desire to desire.

Past to present.

Still holding her to him, Jake kissed her long and hard, until she began to move against him, seeking, needing. Then he rolled her onto her back, settling himself between her thighs. She reached for him, urging him to take her, to fill her, and when he did, her body bowed, begging for more. They began moving together until it was impossible to know who was giving and who was taking, and in the end, they tumbled into oblivion together.

Still a little breathless, Jake propped himself up on one elbow and gazed down at a drowsy Annabelle, her eyes closed. "Marry me, Anna."

Annabelle's eyes flew open.

"No." He put a finger over her lips when she started to speak. "You're already thinking of all the reasons why you shouldn't, so don't say anything yet. Just listen." His fingers skimmed over her cheek, then down over the swell of each breast. "I know you're starting this business and you've got a lot on your plate, but I want to help. And I don't mean by trying to tell you how to run the business. I mean by supporting you in every way possible. You want me in here hanging wallpaper, I'm your man. You want me to butt out and stick to police work... Well," he admitted, grinning, "that might hurt my feelings, but I'll live." He lifted one of her slender hands to his lips, and kissed it. "So long as you live with me. And if you think the boys will present a problem, I can tell you right now, Ty thinks you're just about the neatest thing since sliced bread. As for Cade... I think he likes me. I think we could be friends. We could be a family, Anna.''

She stared at him, torn between wanting to throw her arms around his neck and tell him yes, a thousand times yes, and wanting to cry. Crying was her only real choice.

"Don't be scared, Anna. We could make it work.''

"I'm...I...Jake, I wasn't expecting a proposal.''

"Honestly, I hadn't intended on asking so soon. It just sort of popped out, but it's right. It's what I want. The question is, what do you want?''

"I'm not sure.'' That was probably the biggest lie she'd ever told, and she prayed, under the circumstances, God would forgive her.

She was killing him bloodlessly, but he wasn't going to give up. "All right. I can live with that. For now,'' he said, ignoring the dull ache around his heart.

"But tonight changes everything.''

"Not unless you want it to.'' He leaned down and kissed her softly on the mouth. "I wish we had the rest of the night, but—''

"Oh,'' she said. "What time is it?''

"We've got just about enough time to put ourselves back together before we pick up the boys.'' Reluctantly, he sat up and reached for his clothes. His back was to her and it was just as well, he thought, because he couldn't have hidden the disappointment in his eyes. Or the pain.

DRESSED IN JEANS and a T-shirt, Annabelle wandered into the library from the kitchen the following morning, a mug of steaming coffee in her hand. It was Saturday and Cade was still asleep by the fireplace.

She stopped and stared at the sleeping bag where she and Jake had made love last night. Images flashed through her mind of the two of them touching each other, loving each other. It had been like stepping back in time, their bodies almost as attuned to each other as when they were young and recklessly in love.

Recklessly in love. Isn't that exactly where she was now? In love? Certainly. She'd never stopping loving him. Reckless? Unquestionably. And last night was living proof. Why hadn't she had enough courage to stop him? She'd known from the moment he'd said, "Let me love you," where they were headed, yet any protest was weak at best because she'd wanted it to happen, had longed for it to happen. She could have easily stopped things by telling him the truth, but she chickened out. And afterward, when he asked her to marry him, she should have told him then, but, oh, no. She'd wimped out again.

God, what a mess she had made of things. Her selfishness had only created more pain. Already she dreaded the next time she and Jake would be together. When she had told him that last night changed everything, she hadn't realized just how true those words were. But despite that, in her heart she knew she wouldn't do anything differently if she had the chance. She took a step restlessly toward the fireplace and a board creaked loudly. Cade groaned, blinking his eyes open.

"Hey, Mom."

"Good morning. How did you like the first night in your new home?"

"S'great." He yawned. "Got anything here to eat?"

"Atta boy. Now I know you're awake. There's cereal in the kitchen and milk in the cooler."

"Cocoa Puffs or Lucky Charms?" he asked, coming out of the sleeping bag with a long stretch.

"One of each. And you need to hurry. The carpenters will be here—"

She was interrupted by a knock on the door. "That may be them." But when she opened the door, she found Jake and Ty on the front step.

"Good morning," they chorused.

Holding two tall cups of coffee in his hands, Jake nodded toward the bakery box and sack Ty held. "Doughnuts. Cream-filled and chocolate-covered."

"Terrific," Cade said from behind her. "C'mon in."

"And cinnamon rolls and orange juice," Ty announced, slipping between Jake and Annabelle to follow Cade.

Once they were out of sight and earshot, Jake gazed into Annabelle's eyes and said, "When I woke up this morning, I was afraid I had dreamed last night."

"I think I had the same dream."

He smiled. "Some dream, huh?"

She sighed. "What am I going to do with you?"

"We'll go into that in detail later," he said, stepping inside.

With a quick glance in the direction the boys had gone, he pulled her to him and he kissed her soundly. "Now, that's the way to start the day." And he headed for the kitchen with the coffee.

Annabelle watched him amble across the unfurnished foyer, filling it up with his presence the same way he had filled up her life. Might as well avoid the rush and start missing him now, she thought, very much afraid that when he left, she would never be able to fill the emptiness. She followed him through the house, knowing that even these few moments together were precious, regardless of how painful they might be later on.

"Well, I hate to leave good company, but duty calls," Jake said, after he'd finished a second cup of coffee.

Her heart almost skipped a beat. "Nothing...bad, I hope."

"Actually, this may turn out to be one of the good times. For a lot of people, including your cousin Shelby."

"Shelby? How on earth is she involved with police work?"

"She's been conducting an investigation on behalf of one of her clients."

"Joanna mentioned something about an investigation."

Jake nodded. "Well, I can't tell you any details, but I can tell you that it looks like Shelby has stumbled onto some big time graft."

"Really?"

"I would love to make plans with you for tonight," he said, lowering his voice.

"That's okay. I know you've got your job to do." She hated to admit she was grateful for the out.

"You don't get off that easy," he teased her.

As she smiled up at Jake, she feared his words would be a stunningly accurate prediction. She wasn't going to get off easy at all.

"C'mon. Walk me outside."

His cruiser was parked right beside the oak. He climbed in, then stuck his head out of the window. "If

I can make it, I'll be back when your furniture arrives. In the meantime, check the mailbox."

"The mailbox," she repeated, watching him drive away. "What—" She turned around, and there, tucked into the knothole was a piece of paper. She pulled it from its niche and unfolded it.

A,

Been a long time since my last note. I love you more now than I did then. Marry me. I won't stop asking until you say yes.

J

She refolded the note and slipped it into her back pocket. Then she wiped the tears on her cheek and went back inside.

Ty stayed behind with a promise to his father not to overdo things, and Annabelle threatened dire consequences if he broke the promise. The carpenters arrived and went to work upstairs. By midmorning she had both of the boys doing assigned tasks and she was back at work cleaning the wood paneling in the foyer. She had just climbed an eight-foot ladder to reach the crown molding when the doorbell rang.

"Coming," she called, scrambling down from the ladder. "Just hang on, I'm coming." She opened the door, surprised to find her brother. "Drew."

"Hey, sis. Thought I'd come by and see this work in progress."

"I'm glad you did. Come on in," she invited, closing the door behind him.

"Holy cow. There's enough wood on these walls to keep Belle Terre in firewood for the winter," he quipped, looking around at the paneling.

"Grab a rag. I could use another pair of hands."

"I'm allergic to hard work, haven't you heard?"

She gave him a love tap on the shoulder. "I'm just glad you came by, considering."

"Considering what?"

"Haven't you talked to Daddy?"

"Not in a couple of days. I've been tied up with an offshore deal."

"Oh."

"That's a mighty ominous-sounding 'Oh.'"

"Afraid it's more than that."

"Care to explain—" He was interrupted by the doorbell.

"Wait right there," Annabelle said. She opened the door once more and found a smiling Katherine Beaufort.

"Hi," Annabelle said, delighted to see her.

"I come bearing gifts." Katherine reached over and picked up a huge box leaning against the house.

"Come in. Gifts or not, I'm glad to see you."

"Wow," Katherine exclaimed once she was inside the foyer. "Would you look at the difference. It hardly looks like the same place you—" She stopped upon seeing Drew. "Oh, hello, Mr. Delacroix," she said coolly.

"Ms. Beaufort."

"You two know each other?"

"We've met," Katherine replied, obviously not too thrilled to see him again.

"I hope your business is doing well?" Drew asked.

"Thriving, thank you."

Annabelle glanced from her brother to Katherine and wondered what in the world was going on. She'd never seen Drew so...formal, almost defensive.

Drew smiled. "Well, I just dropped by to see how things were going." He leaned over and gave Annabelle a kiss on the cheek. "So long, sis."

"Bye."

"Sis?" Katherine asked when he was gone. "You're Drew Delacroix's sister?"

"Yes, why?"

"You never mentioned it."

Annabelle shrugged. "It never came up." She frowned. "Does that bother you?"

"Oh, uh, no," she rushed to assure her. "It's just that Mr. Delacroix—Drew—seems so totally different from you that it was a surprise to find out you were related."

"Drew's a very complicated man. It's true he can be standoffish at times, but he's got a good heart."

Katherine smiled tightly. "I'm sure he does. Oh, goodness," she said. "Here I am, standing here chatting, when I haven't even given you your present." She handed the box over. "These are from me with best wishes for your success."

Annabelle smiled as she opened the box. Inside were the two trefoil windows Katherine had been examining the first time they met. "Oh, Katherine. Oh, how wonderful."

"I had them stripped so you can stain them or paint them. Whatever suits you."

"Oh, Katherine, I can't accept these. You love them."

"That's why I want you to have them. Besides, you're the one who gave me the idea of what to do with them, so they should be in your new home."

"Well, you shouldn't have," Annabelle said, then smiled. "But I'm thrilled you did. C'mon. Let's go find the perfect spot for these."

CHAPTER TWELVE

"Mom! Come quick," Cade called from his new bed-room.

Terrified something had happened to Ty, Annabelle raced into the room. "What? What?" she demanded.

Both boys pointed to the television, which had been hooked up only an hour ago.

"They're talking about our cousin Shelby on TV," Cade said, excitedly.

Annabelle stepped farther into the room in order to see. The face of a local newscaster filled the screen as he delivered the six o'clock news.

"Yeah. It's a big bust," Ty added. "The feds are in on it and everything."

"According to New Orleans Chief of Police—"

As the camera focused on the head of the New Orleans Police Department, they caught a glimpse of Jake standing in the background with some other officers.

"Hey, there's my dad!" Ty exclaimed and was immediately shushed.

"Dr. Carl Lee Shivley, city medical examiner, and chief of staff at the local hospital, has been arrested tonight on charges of falsifying medical records regarding a case involving a prominent businessman, Lyle Masson, and his wife, Connie. Two years ago the Massons' nine-year-old daughter was killed in an accident in which Mrs. Masson was driving the car.

Sources have now confirmed that although Mrs. Masson was intoxicated when the accident happened, Dr. Shivley deleted that information from hospital records. Police are looking into the possibility that Lyle Masson may have paid Shivley as much as ten thousand dollars to falsify those records.

"Authorities have been investigating the possibility of bribery for several weeks, and we understand that they have also uncovered evidence that Dr. Shivley may have misappropriated hospital funds and accepted kickbacks from companies doing business with the hospital. Along with these charges, authorities in St. Tammany Parish have been looking into some questionable land deals.

"This information first came to light through the efforts of attorney Shelby Delacroix, and we are awaiting Ms. Delacroix's exit from the hospital in hopes of interviewing her."

"There she is!" Cade yelled.

Annabelle stared as Shelby smiled back at her from the television screen.

"Ms. Delacroix, John Austin, 'Channel 8 News'. Can you tell us what part you played in Dr. Shivley's arrest?"

"Very little."

"But weren't you the one who started digging through files, asking questions?"

"I was merely doing my duty to a client. Dr. Lucas Henderson is the real detective in this case. He discovered some slides containing blood stains that were previously thought to have been destroyed. And he convinced the ER nurse on duty the night Connie Masson was brought into the hospital to testify that Ms. Masson's blood alcohol was definitely over 0.6."

"We understand the client you're referring to is Ms. Yvette Avenall, currently involved in a custody suit with Mr. Masson."

"I can't comment on that," Shelby told the newsman.

"Does this mean you anticipate your client will win the custody case?"

"No comment. Now, if you'll excuse me," she said, and moved out of the camera's focus.

The newscaster looked directly into the camera. "To summarize, Dr. Carl Lee Shivley has just been arrested on charges of bribery with possible charges of misappropriation of funds to follow..."

"Wow," Ty breathed. "They really nailed that guy."

"Yeah," Cade agreed. "Bet your dad has been working on it from the first. Did you know anything about it, Mom?"

"No," Annabelle said. "At least, I don't think so." But she wondered if what they'd just seen had anything to do with the client Shelby had mentioned to her that day in her office. She remembered Shelby saying the woman had been terrified of her child spending time with the wife of the child's father. Was Yvette Avenall the runaway client Shelby had mentioned? One thing Annabelle did know. As she watched the police haul a bedraggled-looking Dr. Shivley out of the hospital and shove him into a police car, she was glad that there had been no violence. Glad that Jake was safe.

THE NEXT AFTERNOON Annabelle tried to reach Shelby at home, then finally tracked her down at the office.

"Congratulations, cousin," she said.

"Oh, Annabelle, thanks. Believe it or not, I had planned on calling you, but I've had one phone call after another ever since I got here this morning."

"Well, it's not every day a Delacroix makes the six o'clock news. I'm sure everyone wanted to offer their congratulations."

"You're the one who deserves the credit. Honestly, Annabelle, if I hadn't talked to you that day about my client, I'm not sure this would have turned out as well as it did."

"Shelby, I may have sparked an idea in your head, but you're the one who followed up and made it turn out right. I don't understand exactly what all of this has to do with your client, but I hope it means she'll be able to come back and deal with the custody suit now."

"As a matter of fact, she saw the broadcast and called me late last night."

"Will she get custody of her child?"

"I think so now. You see, she knew Masson's wife was an alcoholic, and just as you suggested, she was terrified for her child to be around the woman. She also knew the wife was driving drunk when she had the accident that killed her daughter two years ago. Shivley thought he had covered his tracks so well that no one would be the wiser. He also thought he had the nursing staff so cowed, none of them would dare dispute his word."

"Thank goodness that nurse had the nerve to stand up and tell the truth."

"You're telling me. Her testimony, plus the paper trail of falsified documents, will be more than enough to convict Shivley."

"Well, I just wanted to tell you how proud I am of you."

"Thanks, but I'll accept your praise only if we can have a nice long lunch soon."

Annabelle laughed. "All right. I'll call you next week and we'll pick a time."

"You got it."

WHEN SHELBY HUNG UP the phone, she smiled to herself. Family, she thought. Her grandfather and her great-uncle Philip might have split their family tree, so to speak, all those years ago in a feud over who knew what, but at least it hadn't kept the younger generation from staying close.

She glanced over at the package resting on the corner of her desk. It had arrived by courier a couple of days ago from her aunt Toni. She knew what the package contained.

Hamilton Delacroix's files. And among them were personal notes on his last case, the murder trial of Travis's great-aunt, Camille Gravier.

Now that the investigation of Connie Masson was over, and Yvette was on her way back to Bayou Bel tane, Shelby had to admit she would like nothing better than to dig into the files and satisfy her curiosity. Her fingers fairly itched to thumb through her great-grandfather's papers. She had promised Aunt Mary she wouldn't open them, but despite that promise, she couldn't help wondering why her great-aunt was so adamant that the files remain sealed. How could anything that happened almost sixty years ago be so important? What possible harm could come of looking at them now? Hamilton Delacroix's reputation was unblem

ished, even though the Gravier case was the only murder case he'd ever lost.

Still...

Shelby's fingers drummed against the top of her
desk. What if there was something in the files that
Travis should know? Even though he had told her
Camille Gravier was a tramp and that her own grandfather, Charles Delacroix, had had nothing to do with
the murder, Shelby wondered if Hamilton's files might
contain new evidence. Didn't she owe it to Travis to
find out? Intrigued, she reached toward the package,
then stopped.

She didn't have time for this now. She had work
stacked up a mile high, and no business even thinking
about satisfying her curiosity until she'd caught up on
her workload. As it was, she would be here late tonight.

No, she thought, putting the package of files into her
desk drawer. She had too much of the present staring
her in the face to waste valuable time dealing with the
past. Her questions would have to wait.

JAKE DECIDED HE'D HAD enough. Anna had successfully avoided him for two days ever since the night of
Shivley's arrest, and he didn't intend to put up with it
another minute. The boys were both in school, he had
some free time, and he was going to find out what the
hell was bothering her.

The roofers were at work when he arrived at the
house, and there was a sparkling forest green Lexus
parked in front. He rang the doorbell, and when there
was no answer, he knocked, then realized she probably
couldn't hear either over the hammering. He walked
around to the back of the house.

Annabelle was in the back yard talking to a man Jake

had never seen before. Tall, broad-shouldered and blond, the man was impeccably dressed, and from the smile on his face, he was definitely enjoying Annabelle's company. Jake had never laid eyes on the guy before, but he took an instant dislike to him. Who was he? And what the hell was he doing schmoozing with Anna?

"Are we about to be arrested?" he asked as Jake approached them.

"What?" Annabelle turned around. "Oh. Hello, Jake."

"I tried the doorbell, but nobody answered."

"We were out here talking, and I guess I didn't hear it. Reed Dureaux, this is Jake Trahan, Bayou Beltane's chief of police."

"A pleasure to meet you, Chief." Dureaux offered his hand and Jake shook it.

"Thanks."

"Reed is interested in the historical significance of the Portier House. He's a client of Katherine Beaufort's and she told him about the house and my plans to renovate."

"Really?"

"My family has always had a keen interest in preserving Louisiana's fine old homes, and when I found myself in the area, I decided to see the Portier House for myself." Dureaux smiled at Annabelle. "I had no idea I would find such a charming lady in the bargain."

Jake recognized the Dureaux name. The family was ten times as wealthy as the Delacroix and were members of the New Orleans' upper crust. A week rarely went by without photographs of at least one or more Dureaux plastered all over the society section of the *New Orleans Times-Picayune*.

"The renovations still have a long way to go," Annabelle explained. "I'm afraid Katherine was too generous with her praise."

"But if I hadn't come, I would have missed the pleasure of making your acquaintance. A tragedy to be sure."

Jake wondered if Dureaux had to spend a lot of time perfecting that stereotypical drawl. The man sounded like an extra in an old B movie on the Civil War. Surely women didn't find that kind of thing attractive?

"I've been trying to convince Annabelle to attend a meeting of our little historical group. We get together once a month at our home in the Garden District."

I just bet you have, Jake thought. "Anna," he said, deliberately using the more familiar version of her name. "Could I speak with you for a moment?"

"Is something wrong? Ty's not ill, is he?"

"Why would you think that?"

"Well, you don't usually just drop in out of the blue. I thought there might be a problem."

Jake glanced sharply at Dureaux. "I hate to interrupt, but this will only take a moment."

"Don't trouble yourself," Reed said. "I must be going." He picked up Annabelle's hand and kissed it, while Jake did a slow burn.

"Thank you so much for stopping by, Reed. And for inviting me to visit your historical gathering."

"If you change your mind, we're meeting in two weeks." He gave her his card. "Call me, please."

"Thank you."

"Chief," Dureaux said politely. Jake merely nodded.

"I've never known you to be so rude," Annabelle said when Reed had gone.

"What the hell was he doing here?"

"I told you. Katherine told him about the house and he wanted to see it."

"That's not all it looked like he wanted," Jake mumbled.

"What?"

"Nothing. Is that what you've been doing for the last two days instead of returning my calls? Entertaining?"

Shocked, she merely glared at him for a moment. "I don't care for your tone." Then she turned and walked into the house.

He caught up with her in the kitchen. "And I don't care for your cold shoulder. What's going on, Anna? Four nights ago we were making—"

"Keep your voice down," she said. "The carpenters are in the next room."

Jake took a deep breath. "I just want to know why you're running away from me. From us?"

"I told you I wasn't sure, and you said you could live with that," she reminded him.

"Not while you're having a good time with some other man." Even he couldn't believe he'd said such a thing. He sounded like an irate lover, at best, a jealous beau.

"You said you wouldn't push me."

"I said a lot of things. Not the least of which is that I love you."

She was totally taken back by his anger. This was her gentle lover, her considerate friend? "And you feel that entitles you to what, Jake? My heart, my time, my unquestioned devotion? I told you that I've had enough domineering men in my life. I meant it."

"Are you comparing me to your father?"

"Of course not." She shook her head. "I don't think we should continue this conversation."

"You say so, and that's it? You put me off and I'm supposed to keep on waiting, being understanding?" Anger, jealousy and desperation rolled up inside of him like a tight fist, until he couldn't think straight. "What? So you can dump me again for the first rich guy who comes along? How long will I have to wait this time, Anna? Sixteen more years?"

She gasped, her eyes filling with tears as she turned to run from the room.

"No, Anna, wait..." Jake swore. God, what a mess he'd made of things. He should go after her and apologize. Then he decided maybe he should wait until he cooled off. Even then she might not forgive him. Not that he would blame her. He turned and stomped out of the house, back to his car.

What the hell had gotten into him, bullying her like that?

In all his years in law enforcement he had never thrown his weight around like he did today. He'd done it because he was jealous.

No. He'd done it because he was scared.

Scared he might lose her. Just like he had before.

It was insane. But there it was. He'd taken one look at Reed Dureaux and seen Neal Rowland instead. All his old insecurities had come back to haunt him. In the blink of an eye he'd seen a glimpse of the past and mistaken it for the present. It wasn't rational, but then, he reminded himself, love seldom was. For all his talk of putting the past behind him, the old fears had dug their hooks into him before he realized it. And he'd made a complete ass out of himself.

Fear. He thought he'd overcome it long ago. But obviously not when it came to loving Annabelle.

He wasn't going to be able to gloss this over with a simple apology and more roses, either. Anna was no pushover. Even after he explained how his emotions had gotten tangled up in old fears, she would see that he wasn't as successful at putting the past behind him as he'd thought. He didn't doubt that she would forgive him, but what worried him was that she might use the incident as another excuse to put distance between them.

He would have to find a way to make her trust him again and all the flowers in the state of Louisiana weren't going to help.

Just then his radio crackled with the sound of Miz Luella's voice.

"Chief?"

He picked up the mike and depressed the receive button. "Go ahead."

"We got a call from one of the maids out at the Delacroix place."

"Which one?"

"Said her name was Mae."

"No. Which Delacroix? Charles or Philip?"

"Oh. The call came from Belle Terre. The maid was going on something terrible about voodoo and retribution for the wicked. I never did get her to tell me what it was all about."

Exactly what Jake wished Miz Luella would do now. "And...?"

"Well, sounds to me like somebody broke in and vandalized the place."

"All right. I'm on my way."

Jake turned his cruiser around and headed for Belle

Terre. Getting down on his knees before Anna and begging forgiveness would have to wait.

BY THE TIME JAKE pulled into the driveway of the Delacroix plantation home, the butler, Clovis, was there waiting. The epitome of the family retainer, Clovis had been at Belle Terre long before Jake was a kid sneaking around the bayou at the back of the Delacroix property, and he didn't appear to have aged a day since then. With almost a courtly bow, the old man directed him to the back of the house, then followed. The first thing he noticed was Philip Delacroix sitting in a chair under the shade of a tree. Two servants were attending to him. For a moment Jake thought the old man might be injured, but as soon as he took a step in that direction, Philip shoved one of the servants aside and stood up.

"It's about time you got here. Fine thing when a man is almost burned alive in his own home."

"Now, now," one of the women said. "You know you got to watch your blood pressure, sir. The doctor told you—"

"Stop hovering."

Over the years Jake had seen Philip Delacroix wielding his power in various forms, from the down-home cracker-barrel method he used to distract voters from the fact of his wealth, to righteous indignation over the state's problems with the educational system, to just plain being mean to people who worked for him. But he had never seen him so agitated, so out of control. If Jake didn't know better, he'd think the old man was scared.

"Are you hurt, Senator Delacroix?"

"I could have been. Clovis," Philip snapped at the servant. "Show Chief Trahan where the fire started."

Jake followed Clovis to the northernmost corner of the veranda, and there, not two feet from the house, was a pyramid of coals, some gone to ash, others still holding up the smoldering stack.

The smell of ginger and cloves was so strong it almost took his breath away.

"You see. You see," Delacroix called from across the veranda. "Deliberately set. I could have been killed."

Jake held up his hand. "Just a moment, please." He stepped back, then carefully bent down, balancing himself on the balls of his feet so as not to disturb the area around the coals any more than possible. Unless he was mistaken, the lingering, pungent odor indicated what the old voodoo believers called extreme fire oil, usually made up of ginger and clove oils and petitgrain. The brew had probably been thrown onto the hot coals, and judging from the pattern of black streaks on the concrete at the base of the house, had splashed onto the wood and started the fire. Fortunately, the blaze had been extinguished before it could do much damage. No one had even called the fire department.

Jake sighed, rubbing the back of his neck. He had lived around talk of voodoo most of his life and knew the majority of it was just that, talk. But there were still plenty of folks who believed in its power even in this day and age. In his experience, the charms and spells that were part of the practitioner's art depended more on the victim's fear than any other power, but at the same time he had to admit he'd seen some unexplained deaths attributed to voodoo.

So, he decided, Philip Delacroix had probably made somebody mad and that person was using voodoo to terrorize him. If Jake's memory served him correctly, the purpose of the extreme fire oil poured over hot coals was to gain strength over the practitioner's victim, rather than to cause physical harm. Somebody was sending the powerful man a powerful message. Jake rose and walked back over to Philip.

"Senator, have you had occasion to fire anyone in the last few days?"

"No."

"Is there anyone in your employ who has recently been turned down for a raise or has any reason to be disgruntled?"

"Forget about my employees. I want to know what you're going to do about this...this vile attack on my property?" Philip demanded.

"I'm going to do everything possible to find out who's responsible."

"I can tell you who's responsible. Desiree Boudreaux, that's who." The real danger was past, but instead of growing calmer, Philip was becoming increasingly agitated.

"Why would that old swamp woman want to do something like this?"

"Because she's evil, that's why. She's mean and evil, and she wants to hurt me."

"Does she have any reason to want to hurt you, Senator?" When Delacroix only glared at him, Jake continued. "Do you have any proof that it was Desiree Boudreaux who caused this fire?"

Philip was mopping his face with a handkerchief. "Getting proof is your job, Trahan, not mine. That's what the taxpayers expect, and I—" he poked his own chest "—am just about the biggest taxpayer in the whole damn parish, so that makes me your boss. Now, I want you to stop asking me stupid questions. Get off your butt, and arrest Desiree Boudreaux. Today!'' He stomped across the veranda and into the house.

Jake counted to ten, reminding himself that he was a public servant. As an officer of the law, he couldn't afford to allow his job to become entangled with his personal feelings. And it just plain wouldn't be cricket to punch the lights out of a man more than forty years his senior, no matter how bad he wanted to.

His temper under control, he followed Delacroix into the house. Careful to keep his voice calm, but firm, he said, ''Senator Delacroix, you may be one of the biggest taxpayers in the parish, but that does *not* mean I answer to you. And I have no intention of arresting Ms. Boudreaux, or anyone else, without evidence.''

''I tell you, she's guilty.''

''Do you have a witness?''

''You know damned good and well I don't. That old woman has been living in the swamp so long she knows every trick in the book when it comes to sneaking around and hiding herself.''

''If you honestly think Desiree Boudreaux had anything to do with this incident, I'll question her and—''

''Good Lord, the smell is awful.'' Coughing, Philip whipped out a handkerchief from his suit pocket and put it to his nose. ''Everything is ruined. Clovis!'' he called, his voice muffled through the handkerchief. ''Get me some water. The whole place smells like smoke.''

Maybe counting to twenty would do it, Jake thought, then again, maybe not.

''I'm sorry about your loss, Senator, but I'm sure you have ample insurance coverage. I know that doesn't make up for the hassle—

Philip removed the cloth. ''Insurance.''

"I mean, I assumed—"

"That's what you're really worried about, isn't it? You want to be sure I've got enough coverage so that when you marry my daughter and worm your way into this family, you'll still have it all when I die."

Dumbfounded, Jake simply stared at him for a second before the full implication of Philip's words hit him. If he counted to a hundred, it wouldn't give him enough time to cool down. Enough was enough. "Now, just a damn minute, Senator. I'm trying very hard—"

"To finally get your hands on the Delacroix money. That's what you've been trying to do all along, isn't it? Well, it didn't work sixteen years ago, and it's not going to work now. I intend to cut Annabelle out of my will. She won't get a dime! And not one possession out of this house."

Jake swallowed the words he desperately wanted to say. This was Annabelle's father, and even though they were estranged at the moment, he knew that could change and he didn't want to say anything he couldn't take back later.

"I'm sorry you feel that way, Senator. And as far as the Delacroix money is concerned, I can't speak for Anna, but I can tell you one thing for certain. I didn't want your money sixteen years ago, and I don't want it now. All I care about is making your daughter happy."

"Oh, yes," Philip all but snarled. "Such a pretty speech. But you forget, I've heard it before. And I'm not any more impressed now than I was then."

"You're right," Jake said. "It is the same speech. And Annabelle's still the sweetest, most caring and honest person I've ever known. She's still the best thing that ever happened to me, and I was a fool to lose her. But the difference now is that I'm smart enough not to give up. Smart enough to fight for what I want. I love her, and I want to spend the rest of my life with her. And Cade.''

Suddenly Philip's eyes sparked, and his mouth curled at the edges in a thin smile. "Yes, Cade. We mustn't forget about Cade.''

Casually, as if it were the only thing of importance, he walked over to a set of three crystal decanters and liqueur glasses sitting on a silver tray. After removing the top from one of the decanters, he poured what appeared to be sherry into a liqueur glass.

Jake didn't like the sudden change in the Senator's demeanor. One minute he looked as if he were about ready to explode, and the next he looked like the cat that swallowed the canary. What in the world was going on with Delacroix?

"I haven't forgotten about Cade,'' Jake said. "He's a wonderful kid. Bright and compassionate. I hope someday he'll come to think of me as a father.'' Jake didn't really know why he was bothering to say all this to Delacroix, except perhaps that since he hadn't stood up for loving Anna all those years ago, and he somehow needed to make up for it now.

Philip sipped his sherry. "So you think Annabelle is honest and caring, do you?''

"She is.''

"She's a liar.''

There was a sofa separating him from the old man, and it was all Jake could do not to vault that sofa and choke the hell out of Philip Delacroix. He clenched his fists at his sides. "I'll send one of my men back out here to take your statement,'' he said flatly, and started for the door. "I think it would be better—"

"She cheated you, Jake."

At that, Jake stopped and turned. "Senator Delacroix, at the moment, the badge pinned to my shirt is the only thing keeping me from smashing in your face. But I'm warning you. Don't push me."

"Ask her."

The look in Delacroix's eyes was so sadistically gleeful it made Jake's blood run cold. Had the old man gone crazy?

"Ask her what she took from you sixteen years ago. What little secret she's been keeping all this time."

The hair stood up on the back of Jake's neck and fear knotted his stomach. A small voice of warning told him to run. Leave, before he regretted staying. He hated himself for forming the question in his mind, let alone voicing it. "What are you talking about?"

"I'm talking about the boy. I'm talking about Cade."

"What about him?"

"Haven't you wondered why Rowland divorced her? Why he never contacts Cade?"

Before Jake could respond, Philip, still wearing the same sadistic grin, raised his glass in salute. "Fifteen years late, but what the hell. Congratulations, Daddy," he said. "It's a boy."

CHAPTER THIRTEEN

IT CAN'T BE TRUE.

That phrase kept bouncing around in Jake's brain as he drove away from Belle Terre.

Annabelle wouldn't have kept something so important from him all these years. She wouldn't have married another man while carrying his child. They had been so desperately in love with each other. So committed to each other. They had even planned to elope the very night Philip Delacroix had come to him with the news that Anna was marrying Neal Rowland.

No. He shook his head in denial. It just wasn't possible.

It couldn't be true.

But what if it was?

The realization that Cade might indeed be his struck Jake, in a kind of delayed reaction. The idea was so startling, so overwhelming that he actually slammed on the brakes of the cruiser.

Thank God he hadn't reached the main road back into town and there were no cars to be seen. Confused and trembling, he pulled to the side of the road and turned off the engine. He had to try to make some sense out of all this. As he grasped the steering wheel in a white-knuckled grip, Cade's face swam before him. In his mind's eye he studied it, comparing it to his own. Since Cade had had his head shaved, it was difficult to remember exactly what his hair had looked like. Jake recalled it was sun-streaked. Would it grow out dark brown like his and Ty's now that he was away from the Florida sun? When he visualized the hair, then the whole face, he saw...

His own eyes staring back at him.

Jake felt as if his heart had skidded to a stop. Oh, God, it could be true. It was true.

And it wasn't just his eyes. The fullness of his lips was like Jake's, the shape of his hands....

His son. Cade was his son!

Why hadn't he see it before? Why hadn't he recognized the same features he saw when he looked at his own reflection in the mirror every morning?

The answer, simple as it was, didn't help much. He hadn't recognized Cade as his because it was the last thing he would ever have suspected.

Or the pain of realizing that Anna had lied to him.

"Oh, Anna," he whispered, leaning his forehead on his hands. "What have you done?"

How could she have kept silent all these years? How could she have passed Cade off as Neal Rowland's son all this time? Cade was his son, and he had missed all of those growing-up years, he thought, remembering how much he'd enjoyed watching Ty grow from toddler to teenager.

Ty.

Ty and Cade were half brothers. The realization left him dazed. How was he going to tell Ty that he had a half brother? And how would Ty react to such news? And Cade? He thought about how close the two boys had become. What would this do to their relationship? For that matter, what would it do to his relationship with Ty, or any relationship he hoped to have with Cade? Everything seemed hopelessly snarled.

He wasn't going to get the answers to any of his questions sitting on the side of the road. There was only one person who could tell him what he wanted to know.

JAKE WAS GRATEFUL that he'd had to return to the station to file a report on the fire at the Delacroix estate. It gave him time to prepare himself before talking with Anna. He couldn't deny he was angry, but storming into her house and demanding answers wasn't the way to handle the situation. For one thing, he couldn't be sure she would be alone. He didn't want to snatch minutes between instructions to carpenters.

Nor did he want Cade present when they talked.

He called home, checking to see if Cade was still there tutoring Ty. Jake wanted to be sure Cade stayed put until he had a chance to speak to Anna. But he didn't expect Cade to answer the phone.

"Hey, Chief," the boy said. "You wanna talk to Ty?"

"Uh, no, I just, uh..." His throat closed with emotion when he realized he was talking to his son, and he coughed to cover the hesitation. "Excuse me. I just wanted to let him know that I would be a little later than I planned. Maybe a half hour to an hour. Why don't you call your mom and tell her I'll bring you home."

"That's okay. My aunt Joanna is picking me up at five-thirty and taking me to dinner with my cousin Nikki."

"Well then...guess I'll see you later. Oh, Cade?" Jake said before he hung up.

"Yeah?"

"Have a good time, okay?"

"Sure. See ya." Jake stared at the phone for several minutes, still trying to assimilate the fact that he had not one, but two sons.

"You done for the day, Chief?" Miz Luella asked.

"Yeah."

"Well, you say hello to Tyler for me."

"Oh, I'm not going straight home. Would you notify dispatch that I'll be at the Portier House for a while, then home."

Miz Luella smiled. "My goodness gracious, but you're spending an awful lot of time over there lately. They just don't come any sweeter than Annabelle." She winked at him. "But then, I reckon you already know that."

Jake smiled. "Good night, Miz Luella."

"'Night, Chief."

As he watched his secretary walk out of the office, he was reminded of yet another factor in the mess of tangled lies and lives.

Gossip.

What was going to happen when news of Cade's paternity hit the grapevine? There were plenty of narrow-minded people who would be ready and willing to censure the child for mistakes made by his parents. Jake was determined to prevent that if he could. The degree of negative fallout from this situation would depend on Annabelle and her reaction when she discovered he knew about Cade.

He got up, pushed his chair back and walked out of his office. It was time to face Annabelle. Time to face the truth.

HUMMING ALONG to a popular country-and-western song wafting from the portable radio, Annabelle was in the middle of emptying boxes of books when she heard the doorbell ring. Wiping her dusty hands on the seat of her jeans, she hurried to answer it.

"Jake," she said, surprised to see him.

"May I come in?"

She opened the door and he stepped inside. He looked tired, she thought. It had only been hours since their disagreement, but she had certainly felt the strain. She wondered if he had, too.

"I'm glad you came back." When he didn't respond, she frowned. She was trying to make it easier for both of them to get past what had happened today. Even though he had said some hurtful things, after he'd gone, she realized that she could have handled the situation better.

"When I left here I got a call," he told her. "There was a small fire at Belle Terre."

"I hope no one was hurt. Drew wasn't home, was he?"

"No." When she said nothing further, he added, "No one was hurt, including your father." Now that he was face-to-face with her, he had no idea what to say, and he admitted that part of him wanted to believe Philip, not Anna, was the liar.

"But I'm sure he had the staff jumping through hoops, waiting on him hand and foot. My father has a way of taking any situation, no matter who's involved, and making himself the center of it. Believe me, his selfishness knows no bounds. I've only just realized to what extent he's willing to go to get his way. My sister warned me. Even Drew. It's taken me a lot of years to see my father for who he really is. My only regret is that I didn't see it sooner.''

"Sixteen years sooner?"

Something—the tone of his voice, perhaps, or the set of his jaw—told her his question wasn't curiosity. Her heart beat wildly in her chest as she looked into his eyes and saw the pain and anger in their depths. He knew.

And there was only one other person who could have told him.

He knew, and he hated her for it. That, too, was in his eyes.

She took a deep breath. "Yes. If I'd known what kind of person he was all those years ago, my life would have been very different."

"And mine?" After a long silence, he added, "And Cade's?"

Annabelle closed her eyes. So, at last it was over. No more lies. But how much more pain? She opened her eyes and looked straight at Jake.

"Yes."

"He's mine?"

"Yes."

He had thought he was prepared to hear her admit the truth, but it still hit him like a fist to his gut. "Just a little something you neglected to mention when you came back to town? Were you ever going to tell me? Or were you just going to go on living a lie for the rest of your life?"

She had always expected him to be angry. He had a right to be. And she had always expected to be over- whelmed by guilt, to the point that she had been pre- pared to take his wrath because she deserved it. Now that the time had come, she was amazingly calm. And strong.

"Can we go into the library and at least sit down to discuss this?" She didn't wait for his answer, but turned and walked into the other room.

"What is there to discuss?" he said, following her. "You know, I don't know which is worse. Lying to me, or lying to Cade. For God's sake, Anna. He's my son."

"And mine," she said, taking a seat on the sofa.

"And you've had him all to yourself for fifteen years!" he exploded. "How could you do this? How could you keep him from me? How could you let him grow up thinking another man was his father?"

She let him spew out his anger, knowing they wouldn't be able to talk reasonably until he did. She was still astounded that her worst nightmare had come to pass and she had survived it. Even more amazing was that all her fear was gone. Years of dread had slipped away as if Jake had pulled a plug and it had drained out of her. No matter what happened now, she would face it. She would survive.

When he finally sighed and asked, "Did Rowland know?" she knew he was ready to hear her answer.

"Not at first. Two years ago Cade was in a car accident and Neal found out Cade's blood type didn't match his or mine. Of course he confronted me, and I admitted the truth. I thought for a while that we might still be able to make the marriage work, but it was no good." She looked up at Jake. "Neal could never forgive me."

He sat down beside her. "Why, Anna? Why didn't you come to me when you first knew you were pregnant?"

"I was going to. In fact, I had my bags packed, ready to walk out the door."

"What stopped you?"

"Not what, who. My father caught me sneaking out of the house and demanded the truth. He insisted I have an abortion."

Jake's head snapped around. If he hadn't already hated Philip Delacroix, he did now. "Why didn't you?"

"Because I loved you, and it was your baby."

"Then why—"

"Because I didn't have the guts to stand up to my father," she said, her voice shaking. "I don't even know if I can explain it to you. It all sounds like a pitiful excuse now, but I depended on him. When my mother left, she took Joanna with her, but not me. She abandoned me, Jake. My father was all I had."

"You had me."

"I thought so. Until my father convinced me otherwise. He told me that you were only interested in the Delacroix money. He convinced me that it would ruin his political career to have a daughter married one jump ahead of the doctor, and—"

"But that's exactly what you did do. With Rowland. How did you pull it off?"

"I—I'd dated Neal a few times before you and I started seeing each other. He kept calling me all along."

"You never told me."

She looked into his eyes. "Because it wasn't important. Neal wasn't important."

"Then—"

"Daddy kept after me to go out with him. Neal was in college, working toward a business degree, Daddy said I was a fool not to see what a great future I could have with him. He didn't mention that Neal saw me as just as much of a political asset as Daddy saw him. He was only too happy to step into the picture. I've always suspected Daddy offered some extra enticements, considering Neal got such a fat offer from a very prominent brokerage firm in Florida right after he graduated from college.''

She sighed. ''I was only a few weeks pregnant and Daddy made sure Neal wasted no time in sweeping me off my feet and into a quick marriage. Neal's parents were set to spend three months in Europe, so we had a small ceremony in their home before they left.''

''And Rowland never suspected?''

''I always thought he did, but as long as he wasn't faced with the truth, he could ignore it. When Cade was in that accident, he couldn't ignore it anymore.''

''And you went along with all of it. You let your father rearrange your whole life to suit his purposes.''

''Don't you see, Jake? I let him convince me because I didn't have the courage to stand up for you, for our love. He counted on my dependence, just like he counted on your low self-esteem. He used us both, without any consideration for our feelings or Cade's. As long as the Delacroix name and fortune were intact, he didn't care.''

''But as soon as Rowland found out, there was no need for you to continue the charade. Why didn't you contact me? Why didn't—''

''You were happily married, Jake. Or at least, so I thought. What was I supposed to do? Walk back into your life and say, 'Oh, by the way, you're the father of my son?' I didn't even know you were living in Bayou Beltane again until the day you stopped me after running that red light. Or that your wife had died and Ty was sick. I knew none of it.''

"Why haven't you told me since then? Anna, we made love on this very floor. Why didn't you tell me then?"

"I wanted to. I planned to." When he looked away, she knew he didn't believe her. "What do you want me to do, Jake? Tell you I'm sorry? I am. You want me to say it was the biggest mistake of my life? It was. You want me to say I wish I could change it? Of course I do. But I can't. Even blaming my father doesn't do any good, because it won't give you the years you lost with Cade, or the years he lost with you. It won't give us back the life we might have had.''

"I just wish you'd been honest with me from the beginning.''

"So do I. But since we're being honest now, why didn't you fight for me, Jake?''

"This isn't about me—''

"It's about both of us. It took my father hours to convince me not to marry you. How long do you think it would have taken you to change my mind? I can tell you. A minute. Seconds. Where were you, Jake?''

When she finished, she felt spent, all her energy gone. All that was left was for her to say one last thing. "I don't know what happens now. I only know I love you. I've always loved you. If that's not enough, then…''

He was silent for several minutes, then stood up. "Are you going to tell Cade?''

The fact that he would have to ask was more painful than she could ever have imagined. "Of course.''

"I'd like to be there when you do tell him.''

"Of course.''

He stared down at her for a moment, then shook his head. "I don't know what happens now, either." Then he walked out.

JAKE DIDN'T GET MUCH sleep that night. He tried, but it was pointless. All he could think about was the wasted years and that he had a son who didn't even know he was his father. Anna had robbed him of those years. Robbed Cade of his real father. If he could go back and start over...

Then something Annabelle had said made him stop and think about being so eager to place blame.

Where were you, Jake?

Recalling that night, he thought about his reaction when Delacroix had informed him Annabelle didn't want to have any more to do with him. The shock had quickly given way to anger and self-pity. He had never really questioned the abruptness of Annabelle's decision to leave him for Neal Rowland. If he had been thinking with anything but his wounded ego and pride, he might have even considered the possibility of pregnancy. But he hadn't. He'd been too busy licking his wounds and feeling sorry for himself.

Not a pretty picture, he decided, gazing out at the new day.

Anna was right. Neither of them had stood up for their love. Neither of them had been able to sacrifice for the other.

"What's happening?" Ty said, wandering into the kitchen. "You going out on a call?"

"No. Restless, I guess." Jake poured himself another cup of coffee.

Ty yawned. "I'm hungry." He went to the cupboard, removed the cereal and fixed himself breakfast. "Want some?"

"No thanks. Can we talk?" Jake asked when Ty was seated at the serving counter.

"Shoot."

"You and Cade have gotten pretty tight, haven't you?"

"Yeah. He's great."

"Then you wouldn't mind if he was around a lot more?"

Ty stopped eating. "You mean, like all the time?"

"Well, I—"

"I knew it. I just knew it." A big smile spread across Ty's face. "You're gonna ask Cade's mom to get married, aren't you?"

Jake was stunned that Ty had automatically leapt to that conclusion.

"Listen, Dad. If you're worried about how I feel, because of Mom and everything, you don't have to worry. Nobody can take Mom's place. But Miz Rowland is really neat. I wouldn't mind having her for a stepmother. And the coolest part is that Cade and I would be sorta like brothers." He took a bite of cereal, chewed twice and swallowed. "But I guess the important thing is that you love her, huh?"

Before Jake could answer, the phone rang.

"Hello?"

"Chief, this is dispatch. We've got a 911. Paramedics are on the scene. Victim fell off a ladder. The son asked us to notify you."

"Me?"

"Said his name was Cade Rowland."

THE PARAMEDICS HAD PACKED up and were just leaving when Jake and Ty arrived. The ambulance crew stopped long enough to give them the news that there was no concussion, only a nasty bump on the head and a small cut. Jake and Ty found Annabelle sitting on the sofa in the library with Cade standing beside her. She glanced up, tears in her eyes.

"I asked Cade not to call you."

"Are you okay?" He brushed a wayward strand of hair from her cheek.

"She was up on that ladder." Cade pointed to the eight-footer leaning against one of the shelves. "I told her to wait until I got up, but—"

"It's all right, Cade," Jake assured him. "Your mother has a mind of her own."

"You're tellin' me," the teenager replied.

"Why don't you go ahead and get ready for school. Ty, you can go with him. I'll stay with your mother."

Cade shrugged. "Suits me."

"Jake—"

He nodded toward the boys, indicating for her to wait till they were out of the room.

"Now," he said when they were gone. "What the hell were you doing up on that ladder at this hour of the morning?"

"I couldn't sleep, so I decided to tackle unpacking more books."

He touched the bandage on her forehead. "You sure you're okay?"

She nodded, then had to close her eyes against the flash of dizziness. "Just a king-size headache." When she opened her eyes again, Jake was staring at her.

"You scared the hell out of me," he whispered.

"I'm sorry."

He put a finger to her lips. "No more apologies

Well…just mine. I'm sorry, Anna. You were right about everything last night. We're both responsible for what happened in the past, but we've paid the price. We can start over now.''

"I—I thought you'd never be able to forgive me. That you'd stopped loving me. I thought—''

"Stopped loving you? I might as well stop breathing. I admit finding out I was Cade's father was a shock, and I was angry—''

"You have every right to be.''

He shook his head. "I don't want to be angry, or right. I want you, Anna. And I want both of my sons.'' He pulled her into his arms.

"I love you.''

"Oh, Jake. I love you so much.'' She kissed him. "So much.''

"I told you once that not many people get second chances, and I was right. This is ours, Anna. Yours, mine, Cade's and Ty's. We can't let it slip away.''

"You really think we can make it?''

"You can bet on it. And the first step is telling the boys,'' he said, holding her tight.

Annabelle leaned back in his arms. "Yes. And I don't think we should wait.''

As much as Jake wanted Cade to know they were father and son, now that the moment was at hand, he suddenly had an attack of nerves. "How do you think he'll take it?''

"I don't have any idea. I know he likes you and respects you.

"What about Ty? How do you think this will affect him?''

Jake rested his forehead against hers and smiled.

"He thinks I should ask you to marry me, and that you'd make a great stepmom."

Annabelle's heart swelled with love. "I think he'd make a wonderful stepson."

"It's no good trying to predict how either of them will react," he said. "The only way to find out is to tell them."

"Now?" she whispered.

"Now. Do you want me to do it?"

"No. I have to be the one to tell Cade."

"All right." He gave her a long, sweet kiss, full of promise and commitment, then he took her hand. "Boys," he called. "Can you come in here?"

A few seconds later both boys came into the room, dressed for school. "We're ready," Ty said, hefting his backpack onto one shoulder.

"Uh, yeah," Jake began, "Anna and I need to talk to you. Cade, will you sit next to your mother? Ty, over here." He pointed to the settee opposite the sofa.

Cade and Ty exchanged what's-up glances, then took their appointed seats.

"Something wrong?" Cade asked.

"Not wrong, exactly," Annabelle said, turning on the sofa to face her son. "Cade, I have something to tell you, and I honestly don't know how to make you understand…I think I need to start at the beginning." She looked at Jake and saw so much love shining in his eyes, it gave her sagging courage a boost.

"When we—Jake and I—were in high school, we dated. In fact, we were in love." She watched as Cade's eyes widened, and waited for him to absorb this first all-important hurdle.

"Very much in love," Jake added.

Annabelle smiled. "Yes. But we had to keep our love a secret."

"Why?" Cade asked logically.

"Because of your grandfather. He didn't think Jake was good enough to date, much less marry, a Delacroix." When Cade opened his mouth to ask another question, Annabelle raised her hand. "I know you've got questions, but I think most of them will be answered by the time I finish.

"As I said, we were very much in love, and we planned to elope. On the night we were going to get married, Daddy caught me sneaking out of the house and stopped me. I told him how much I loved Jake, and begged him to let me go, but he refused. I told him that I had to go." She looked her son in the eyes. "I told him that I was pregnant with Jake's child. He wanted me to have an abortion, but I refused." She reached out and took Cade's hand. "I loved Jake, and I loved his child. There was no way I was going to give it up."

She watched as Cade's gaze went to Jake's and stayed there. The pain and confusion in her son's eyes were almost more than she could bear, but she knew she had to go on. "I was barely seventeen, timid, horribly insecure, and more terrified than I can ever explain. My whole life I had depended on my father. He wanted me with him when my mother walked away from us. He protected me, he cared for me. Whatever he said, I did. But I couldn't, wouldn't give up my baby, Jake's baby. Not even for my father. However, your grandfather isn't a man who takes no for an answer. He used my insecurity and played on my guilt, saying that he hadn't abandoned me as my mother had. He finally even convinced me that Jake didn't really love me. That all he wanted was the Delacroix money and prestige.''

"And it was a lie,'' Jake said, taking up his part of the story. Glancing at Ty, he saw that he was as stunned as Cade. "He came to me that same night and told me Anna had decided she was tired of me and that I'd never been good enough for her. He even offered me money to leave town. I left, but not with his money. I was so hurt and angry that I ran off and joined the marines. And I swear, I never knew that she was carrying my child. Not until your grandfather told me yesterday. I would never have left if I'd known."

Jake turned to Ty and put a hand on his shoulder. "That doesn't mean I regret marrying your mother or having you."

The boy gazed up at him with so much compassion, his breath caught. "I know."

Annabelle felt Cade's hand tense in hers. "Daddy arranged for me to marry another man. I didn't want to, but Jake was gone, and my baby needed a father, so I...I gave in and did what Daddy wanted. I married Neal Rowland."

For the last few minutes Cade hadn't taken his eyes off Jake.

Now he looked at his mother. "Dad isn't... You're trying to say that Jake is my...my real father," he finished, his voice almost a whisper.

"Yes."

"Why...why didn't you ever tell me?"

"At first I couldn't. Later, I—I had been living the lie..." This was no time to stumble over the truth, she admonished herself.

"That's not totally true. I was afraid you wouldn't

want to be with me anymore. I was afraid you would never trust me again. Or love me.''

"But Dad—Neal knew, didn't he?''

"He suspected all along, but he didn't know for certain until your accident.''

Briefly, Cade closed his eyes, and released a small sigh. "I always thought he didn't like me. Now I know why.''

Annabelle's heart broke. "Oh, sweetheart, I never wanted you to be hurt. I love you.''

He put his other hand over hers, and when he spoke, he heard the uncertainty in his voice. "What...you know, what happens now?''

"That depends on you,'' Jake said.

"What do you mean?''

"Cade, this was as big a shock to me as it was to you. And Ty, as well. In the last twenty-four hours all our lives have changed. I can't expect you to accept that lightly or quickly. You or Ty. And since we're dealing with the truth here, you might as well know the rest of it. I love your mother and I want to marry her. Now, if you need time to adjust to that, I can understand.''

"Dad?'' Ty asked softly. "Does this mean Cade and I are real brothers?''

"Half brothers, but yes.''

Ty looked at his friend, still a friend, but now so much more.

"If it's okay with you, the half thing gets confusing.'' Ty smiled. "Just 'brother' sounds all right to me.''

Jake, Annabelle and Ty all looked at Cade, waiting

for him to respond. Annabelle held her breath and prayed while his gaze went searchingly from one to the other, finally landing on Ty.

"Yeah," he said at last, his eyes glistening. "Sounds pretty cool to me."

CHAPTER FOURTEEN

"YOU GOT EVERYTHING?" Ty asked his father.

"Think so. Cade, did you deliver the note?"

"Put it right where you told me to."

"Then she got it," Jake said confidently. He and Anna had been leaving notes in their old "mailbox" every day for the last three days. He knew she checked every morning and evening. "Well, how do I look?"

Ty and Cade eyed Jake's new suit. "Want the truth?" Ty asked.

"Be brutal."

Ty held out his hand and rocked it back and forth. "Personally, it's a little dull for my taste. Whatdaya think, bro?"

"Ditto."

"Then it's a good thing neither of you are eloping, isn't it? And don't give Mrs. Segal any grief while we're gone," he warned.

"Yes, sir," they answered.

Jake turned to face his sons. His sons. He still had trouble believing how lucky he was. "You guys don't really mind not being at the ceremony, do you? I mean, you understand that Anna and I want to elope just the way we planned all those years ago?"

"Oh, sure."

"Yeah. No problem."

Jake took a deep breath. "Well," he said. "Guess

I'm ready." He shook both their hands, then picked up his duffel bag and headed outside. Cade caught up with him just as he reached the car.

"Jake?"

"Yeah?"

"Uh..." The boy glanced away, then back at Jake. "I just, uh, wanted to tell you thanks for putting up with me for the last few days. You know, since you found out I was—"

"My son."

"Yeah. I sorta blew my cool a couple of times, 'specially about Granddaddy."

"That relationship may never be what you want it to be, Cade. For you or your mother. I hate that, but I can't say there's any love lost between me and Philip Delacroix."

"Well, anyway, you just let me blow, and didn't get upset or nothing."

"Cade, we're all still adjusting, but together we'll make it."

"I guess so. And I wanted to say that I'm glad you're marrying my mom."

"You mean so you're legal, so to speak?"

"Oh, no. Even if you weren't my real father, I'd still want you to marry her."

Jake smiled. "Thanks."

"You make her happy."

"No happier than she makes me."

When Cade didn't walk away, Jake said, "Something else on your mind?"

"Uh, yeah. When you're, you know, married and everything...I was wondering if it would be all right—and Ty's cool with this, 'cause we already talked—if you would mind if I called you Dad?"

For a moment Jake couldn't speak. When he did, his voice was husky with emotion. "I can't think of a nicer wedding present. Thanks, son."

Cade grinned and ran back into the house.

Five minutes later Jake was standing on Annabelle Delacroix Rowland's doorstep waiting for her to answer. If he'd thought his conversation with Cade had him speechless, it was nothing compared to seeing Anna dressed and ready to marry him.

"I got your note," she said.

"So," he said, finding his voice. "Does that mean yes?"

"Don't you think it's about time?"

With a laugh, he scooped her into his arms and swung her around and around in the middle of the foyer. "Yeah, I do." He set her back on her feet and kissed her soundly. "I love you, Anna. Thank you for giving me another son. Thank you for giving me a new life."

She wrapped her arms around his neck and drew his head down for another kiss. "We've waited so long for this happiness, sometimes I have to pinch myself to believe it's real."

"It's real. We might have missed out on a few years together, but we'll make up for it by loving each other for the rest of our lives."

It was the promise they had already made to each other, the promise they would make in front of a clergyman. Then they would come back to this house to spend their first night as husband and wife. And tomorrow they would bring the boys home. They would be a family.

DELTA JUSTICE

continues with

OVERRULED BY LOVE

by M.J. Rodgers

Logan Weston had never lost a case. And he'd never gotten involved with a client. But his rules might have to change because the enemies of the Delacroix family were determined—and deadly. With Logan's heart—and the life of Joanna's daughter—on the line, would his luck hold out this time?

Available in March

Here's a preview!

DELTA JUSTICE

OVERRULED BY LOVE

THE DOOR TO THE JAIL opened suddenly. Logan and
Joanna turned toward it as Nikki came through, Chief
Jake Trahan by her side.

"She's all yours, Joanna," Jake said.

From the expression on Trahan's face, Logan had
the distinct impression that the man was doing his job
but took no satisfaction in it.

Logan watched as Joanna moved toward her daughter slowly, hesitatingly, almost as though she were approaching a wild bird that might take wing at any second.

Nikki was five eight, an inch shorter than her mother.
Her long, wavy brown hair was several shades lighter.
Nikki's face was round, her nose a small button, her
large eyes the same walnut brown as her hair.

She did not have Joanna's classic beauty, but she
was a very pretty young woman. And if Logan didn't
miss his guess, behind that hard shell she was project-
ing to the world, a very scared one.

"Let's go home," Joanna said gently.

"Your father has left his limousine here for our
transportation," Logan said. "We have much to discuss."

Joanna turned to him, surprise in both her eyes and
the cool tones of her voice.

"Nikki just spent the night in jail, Mr. Weston. She needs a bath, a hot meal, time to recuperate, a good night's rest. Surely your questions can wait until tomorrow?"

"No, they can't."

"Excuse me?"

"Your concerns as a mother are understandable. But you must understand my concerns as Nikki's attorney. I need to know the facts from her, and I need to know them now."

Logan drew open the door and held it for them. "After you."

Joanna's eyes never left his face. She was measuring him with a hard, focused scrutiny that held nothing back.

She didn't like his insistence on talking to Nikki now. If Nikki had been his daughter, he wouldn't have liked it, either. But Nikki wasn't his daughter. She was his client.

Logan didn't want Nikki rested, recuperated. He wanted her scared. He wanted the smell of the jail and the memory of being behind bars still fresh in her mind. Because if they were, he reasoned, she'd be much more likely to cooperate with him.

Joanna knew what he was doing and why. Logan could read the raw pain of it in those deep blue eyes that stared so straight into his. She had the right to refuse him. Indeed, if it had been his daughter and Joanna had been the attorney making this demand, he might have refused her.

But Joanna didn't refuse. She nodded. Then, with quiet dignity, she led her daughter through the open door of the jail to the parking lot and Philip Delacroix's waiting limousine.

Not for the first time that morning, Logan fervently wished he had met Joanna Delacroix Gideon under different circumstances.

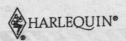

Take 4 bestselling love stories FREE

Plus get a FREE surprise gift!

Special Limited-time Offer

Mail to Harlequin Reader Service®

3010 Walden Avenue
P.O. Box 1867
Buffalo, N.Y. 14240-1867

YES! Please send me 4 free Harlequin Intrigue® novels and my free surprise gift. Then send me 4 brand-new novels every month. Bill me at the low price of $3.34 each plus 25¢ delivery and applicable sales tax, if any.* That's the complete price and a savings of over 10% off the cover prices—quite a bargain! I understand that accepting the books and gift places me under no obligation ever to buy any books. I can always return a shipment and cancel at any time. Even if I never buy another book from Harlequin, the 4 free books and the surprise gift are mine to keep forever.

181 HEN CE69

Name	(PLEASE PRINT)

Address	Apt. No.

City	State	Zip

This offer is limited to one order per household and not valid to present Harlequin Intrigue® subscribers. *Terms and prices are subject to change without notice.
Sales tax applicable in N.Y.

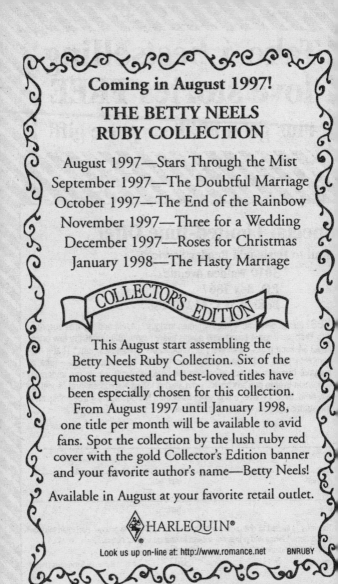

Coming in August 1997!

THE BETTY NEELS
RUBY COLLECTION

August 1997—Stars Through the Mist
September 1997—The Doubtful Marriage
October 1997—The End of the Rainbow
November 1997—Three for a Wedding
December 1997—Roses for Christmas
January 1998—The Hasty Marriage

COLLECTOR'S EDITION

This August start assembling the
Betty Neels Ruby Collection. Six of the
most requested and best-loved titles have
been especially chosen for this collection.
From August 1997 until January 1998,
one title per month will be available to avid
fans. Spot the collection by the lush ruby red
cover with the gold Collector's Edition banner
and your favorite author's name—Betty Neels!

Available in August at your favorite retail outlet.

HARLEQUIN®

WELCOME TO *Love Inspired* ™

A brand-new series of contemporary inspirational love stories.

Join men and women as they learn valuable lessons about facing the challenges of today's world and about life, love and faith.

Available in retail outlets
in January 1998.

LIFT YOUR SPIRITS AND GLADDEN YOUR HEART with *Love Inspired*™!

Steeple
Hill™

LI298

**Cupid's going undercover
this Valentine's Day in**

The Cupid Connection

Cupid has his work
cut out for him this
Valentine's Day with these
three stories about three
couples who are just too *busy*
to fall in love...well, not for long!

**ONE MORE VALENTINE
by Anne Stuart
BE MINE, VALENTINE
by Vicki Lewis Thompson
BABY ON THE DOORSTEP
by Kathy Gillen Thacker**

Make the Cupid Connection this February 1998!

Available wherever Harlequin and Silhouette books are sold.

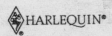 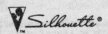

Make a Valentine's date
for the premiere of

◆ HARLEQUIN® **Movies**

starting February 14, 1998 with

Debbie Macomber's

This Matter of

Marriage

on **the movie channel** tmc

...st tune in to **The Movie Channel** the **second Saturday** ...ght of every month at 9:00 p.m. EST to join us, and be swept ...vay by the sheer thrill of romance brought to life. Watch for ...etails of upcoming movies—in books, in your television ...ewing guide and in stores.

...you are not currently a subscriber to The Movie Channel, ...mply call your local cable or satellite provider for more ...etails. Call today, and don't miss out on the romance!

the movie channel tmc

100% pure movies.
100% pure fun.

◆ HARLEQUIN™

*M*akes any time special.™

...lequin is a trademark of Harlequin Enterprises Limited. The Movie Channel is a trademark of
...wtime Networks, Inc., a Viacom Company.

An Alliance Production   HMBPA298

Born in the USA

**BORN IN THE USA: Love, marriage—
and the pursuit of family!**

HARLEQUIN®   Silhouette®

Look us up on-line at: http://www.romance.net

BUS